# Supernatural Devices

A Steampunk Scarlett Novel

Book One

kailin gow

**Supernatural Devices: A Steampunk Scarlett Novel #1**

Supernatural Devices: A Steampunk Scarlett Novel
Published by THE EDGE
THE EDGE is an imprint of Sparklesoup Inc.
Copyright © 2011 Kailin Gow

All Rights Reserved. No part of this book may be reproduced or transmitted in any form or by any means, graphic, electronic, or mechanical, including photocopying, recording, taping or by any information storage or retrieval system, without the permission in writing from the publisher except in case of brief quotations embodied in critical articles and reviews.

For information, please contact:

THE EDGE at Sparklesoup
14252 Culver Dr., A732
Irvine, CA 92604
www.sparklesoup.com
First Edition.
Printed in the United States of America.

ISBN: 9781597480116

Kailin Gow

## DEDICATION

For those who have their eyes on the future, appreciate the past, yet live in the present. For those who are dreamers who do, and doers who dream, this series Steampunk Scarlett is for you.

**Supernatural Devices: A Steampunk Scarlett Novel #1**

# PROLOGUE

"Miss Seely, Miss Seely!"

Scarlett tried very hard not to show too much annoyance at the approach of one of the porters to the tent where she was currently keeping out of the Egyptian sun. No doubt the young man thought that whatever errand her parents had sent him on this time was vitally important.

Scarlett generally thought that her parents' interest in things buried in the ground was rather less important than they tried to make it sound. Father might have come out here to follow in the footsteps of Sir William Petrie, and Mother might have acquired a small obsession of her own with the myths and folklore of the place, but that didn't make the fashion for antiquarianism any more exciting to a girl of seventeen.

Yet they had insisted that it would be a valuable part of her education, and Scarlett had to admit that she had learned a lot out here. It was just that she would much rather have been back in London. In London, things were always happening, and pieces of broken pottery counted for very little. In London, the sun wasn't hot enough to burn a pale skinned blonde like herself every time she stepped out into it.

Oh, Egypt had its compensations. Its monuments were truly magnificent, while the wildlife here was awe inspiring. Scarlett hadn't shot lions or elephants, preferring to paint them the way her parents did, but she had certainly been close to them. She had seen the great Nile crocodiles slide into the water from the banks, and watched the ibis gathering. And being so far from the stuffiness of Society meant that Scarlett could learn what she wanted, rather than merely those things thought appropriate for a young lady of good breeding. Even today, in the brisk modernity of 1890, people could have some very old fashioned attitudes.

### Supernatural Devices: A Steampunk Scarlett Novel #1

It was just that Scarlett knew perfectly well that London held adventures of its own. Adventures that she had heard since she was a little girl from her parents' friend Mr Holmes, and which she had tried to keep up with by having copies of the *Strand* shipped over, letting her read John Watson's accounts of them, even if it was several months behind everyone else. Not that Scarlett was entirely happy with Mr Holmes at the moment. He had made her a promise before she left, and so far, he had not kept it.

"Miss Seely."

Scarlett turned her attention to the young man who had arrived in the tent. "Yes, Akim? Is it about the clock?"

Ah, the clock. Her parents' great find. Six months of work, and their greatest discovery was an elaborate water clock made from silver. It was certainly impressive, and the inscription marking it as sacred to the Egyptian sky-goddess Nut presumably made it important as well, yet Scarlett couldn't help feeling a little resentful towards the thing, given that it was the reason her parents had extended their work here.

"No, Miss Seely. There is a telegram for you. From London."

## Kailin Gow

The young man held out a sealed envelope. It would have been received at the office back in town perhaps yesterday, meaning that whatever information had been so urgent was already out of date. Still, it was better than waiting for a boat to carry a letter. And it was from London.

Scarlett opened it impatiently and read.

*Scarlett,* it read, *I promised before you left for Egypt that I would send for you if ever I had a case that needed the talents of a young lady of good upbringing, rather than my usual collection of Irregulars. Such a situation has now arisen. Please return at once. Sherlock Holmes.*

Scarlett read the message twice more just to be certain. She refrained from letting out a whoop of joy, but only barely. The young porter was watching her, after all.

"Is there a return message, Miss Seely?" he asked.

Scarlett shook her head. "No, but could you tell me where my parents are? I need to speak to them urgently, if I am going to be on a boat today."

Supernatural Devices: A Steampunk Scarlett Novel #1

# CHAPTER 1

When Scarlett and her parents had left London, it had been a city of mists and freezing fogs. Now that winter had given way to spring, however, it was just about possible to make out the sky above as she rode towards Baker Street in the back of a hansom cab. The night was warm. Warm enough that the coat she wore over a simple, dark travelling dress was almost too much.

Scarlett listened to the rattle of the cobbles beneath the wheels, trying to remember some of what Sherlock had taught her. In theory, the different street surfaces of the city were as unique as the new fingerprints that had caused Scarlett such excitement. No one might have been convicted on the strength of them yet, but the idea of such a clear way of solving mysteries was tantalizing.

Though also possibly a little dull. Scarlett had heard the stories of Sherlock and Dr Watson's escapades, and had marvelled at the idea of a science of deduction. She had even spent time trying to perfect the fundamentals of it in preparation for the day when she would be ready to assist with one of those adventures. She didn't want some new science making things too easy. Although secretly, Scarlett suspected that things would never be that easy. Even with such new ideas, there would always be a place for confusion, which was why people like Sherlock would always be needed to cut through it. People like her.

Persuading her parents to let her go had been easier than Scarlett had thought it would be. Apparently, they thought enough of Mr Holmes that he could simply send for their daughter and they would allow it. Or perhaps they had simply sensed how much Scarlett had desperately wanted to go. After all, parents who had thought nothing of taking their daughter to explore the farthest reaches of the Raj and Malaya when she was just a child would hardly balk at the idea of her having an adventure or two in London.

Though they had insisted on one or two precautions. Firstly, a young woman named Miss Pettingell had travelled with Scarlett for most of the way as a companion, taking the boat with her from Alexandria over as far as

### Supernatural Devices: A Steampunk Scarlett Novel #1

Marseilles, then accompanying her on a succession of trains across France to Calais. Only when they had reached Dover had the two parted, with Scarlett completing her journey to London while Miss Pettingell had gone off to see family in Kent. She had been pleasant enough company on the journey, even if her French had not been much use when put beside Scarlett's, meaning that Scarlett had spent most of the trip serving as her translator.

Secondly, and perhaps rather more usefully, her parents had presented Scarlett with a bronze dagger taken from one of their earlier sites, which currently sat at the base of her purse. It was presumably intended to be as much a memento of the time in Egypt as anything, but Scarlett didn't doubt that her parents intended her to use it in her defense if necessary. After all, they were the ones who had insisted that she had learned to fence and to shoot. They were the ones who had occasionally sought out teachers of obscure fighting arts on their travels, and used their money to persuade those teachers to teach Scarlett. No daughter of theirs was going to go undefended in a dangerous world.

**Kailin Gow**

Now, if only they had found some art that made cab rides go faster. The journey back to London had been a long one. Too long, really. It was possible, far too possible, that whatever mystery Mr Holmes had been working on would have been resolved by now, leaving her unneeded once more. Scarlett wasn't going to risk that. She had actually sent her luggage on ahead of her to the family's town house, simply so that she would be able to go straight to Baker Street and save a little time. Mrs Hudson, the landlady of the place, would undoubtedly allow her in, despite the hour.

The hansom came to a halt, and Scarlett alighted, fishing around in her purse for the correct coins with which to pay the driver. That was easier said than done when it was hard to pick apart the francs and centimes from the pounds, shillings and pence by the light of the gas street lamps. Scarlett managed to locate the fare, and she stood there for a moment or two as the cab drove off, staring up at number 221b. Above, the place would undoubtedly be its usual mess, with the remnants of some experiment or other of Mr Holmes' scattered around, and his violin propped carelessly on the mantelpiece. Scarlett had been there

### Supernatural Devices: A Steampunk Scarlett Novel #1

enough times over the years to picture it easily, and the mess had only gotten worse in the months before she and her parents had left for Egypt, after John Watson had moved out to marry his wife Mary.

Of course, Scarlett realized afterwards, it was utter foolishness to just stand there staring, with her purse in her hand like that. Not the sort of thing she would normally have done at all. Her only excuses were the long journey, combined with the joy of finally arriving at the door of her parents' great friend. It still did not excuse the way she made things so very easy for the thief, though.

A hand snatched at her purse, while another pushed her back. Scarlett had good enough reflexes not to stumble, though she wasn't able to catch her assailant in a joint lock, as she briefly intended. Instead, she was left watching as a figure sprinted from the scene.

Scarlett ran after him, of course. She wasn't about to let some ruffian take her things. She was hardly dressed for a pursuit, given the length of her dress, and Scarlett momentarily cursed propriety under her breath as the young man ahead of her started to pull away. She kept running though, refusing to admit that she might not be able to catch him. She would simply have to be patient. Be determined. And if she happened to pass a constable to whom she could shout "Stop, thief!" then that would be so much the better.

Sadly, there didn't seem to be any sign of any constables around, though, and Scarlett suspected that she was rapidly getting to the stage where she was going to have to admit that she wasn't going to catch the thief. How would that look? Her purse taken from her on the very day she was meant to be proving how useful she could be to Mr Holmes? She stayed with the thief a little longer, hoping that perhaps providence would provide a way. Though Scarlett had to admit, she was still more than a little surprised when it did.

A man stepped out of a side street ahead of the thief, sticking out a leg and tripping him neatly, almost casually. As the thief hit the cobbles, the newcomer reached down and plucked the purse from him.

"I would run along, if I were you," he said. The young man who had stolen Scarlett's purse took one look at him and fled, obviously deciding that discretion was the better part of valour.

### Supernatural Devices: A Steampunk Scarlett Novel #1

Scarlett could not blame him. The newcomer was really quite impressively built, as far as Scarlett could tell beneath the elegantly cut expensive suit he wore. He wore his dark hair a little longer than the current fashion. He appeared to be only a little older than her. Perhaps twenty or so. Other details leapt out at Scarlett as she struggled to observe, from the silver cufflinks of his shirt to his delicate, almost feminine hands. It wasn't difficult, and the young man was hardly a chore to look at. Quite the opposite, in fact.

"This is yours, I believe," the young man said, with just a trace of a smile as he held out the purse.

"Thank you, sir," Scarlett replied, taking it and stowing it away safely. She held out her hand, in a move that was probably far too direct for London. "I am Scarlett Seely."

"A pleasure to meet you, Miss Seely." The young man took her hand and bowed low over it to kiss it in the continental fashion, though Scarlett got the feeling that he was simply doing it because he could. "I am Cruces."

"Well, Mr Cruces…"

The young man shook his head. "Forgive me, Miss Seely, but it is simply Cruces. And now, I fear I must be going."

"Why?" Scarlett asked. "You clearly came here for something."

"And how could you possibly know that I am not simply out for a stroll?" Cruces asked.

"Your clothing suggests that you have money, or at least that you want to give that impression," Scarlett explained, "while your shoes do not show signs of having walked far, as they might were you out for a moonlit stroll. Neither suggests that you live in the area. The hour is not quite right for visiting, and this is hardly a quarter of the city noted for great entertainments, so you must be here on business."

Cruces laughed at that, and his features came alive with it. "That could almost pass for the kind of thing a certain consulting detective who lives down the way does. Well done, Miss Seely."

"If you mean Mr Holmes," Scarlett said, "that is who I was intending to visit, before this. Incidentally, I notice you have stopped being overly familiar. Presumably, that is because you no longer wish to unnerve me into running off?"

Cruces held up his hands. "I surrender. Enough. If you are heading for 221b Baker Street, though, perhaps you would allow me to escort you there? I cannot imagine that the thief who had your property before will be back, but the night holds other dangers for a young lady walking alone. It would make me feel… happier."

Scarlett nodded, with another smile. "That would be pleasant."

It was. Surprisingly so. Cruces did not offer his arm, and Scarlet would not have taken it if he had, but the short journey back to Mr Holmes' lodgings felt almost comfortable. Cruces asked what had brought her there, so Scarlett told him that she had recently returned from an expedition to Egypt, and that Mr Holmes was a friend of her family's. Cruces asked her a couple of questions about her time abroad, and Scarlett did her best to answer, telling him of the beauty of the pyramids and the power of the Nile.

"Yet they are not what holds your heart, are they?" Cruces asked her.

## Kailin Gow

Scarlett hesitated briefly, and then shook her head. "They are spectacular, but they are about the past. Everything that will happen there *has* happened. As much as my parents love that, I prefer places that are more about what is happening now."

Cruces looked wistful for a moment. "The past has its moments, Miss Seely. And I believe we are here."

They were. Scarlett went up the steps to ring the bell, and Mrs Hudson answered, scowling at the lateness of the visit as only an old woman could scowl until she saw who it was. Then her face creased into a smile.

"Scarlett, dear," she said in the Scottish accent she had never lost. "I didn't know that you were in England. You must be here to see Mr Holmes. Dr Watson is here as well. Come in, and I'll see if I can't rustle up some supper."

Scarlett nodded. "It's good to see you, Mrs Hudson."

The landlady's eyes skipped past her. "And what about you, young Mr Cruces? Will you be going up to see Mr Holmes too?"

**Supernatural Devices: A Steampunk Scarlett Novel #1**

Scarlett looked around sharply at that as Cruces made a short bow. "If that is all right, Mrs Hudson. I believe Mr Holmes and I may have business to discuss."

## CHAPTER 2

Scarlett did her best to contain her surprise as they headed up to Mr. Holmes' rooms, not asking how Cruces knew the detective, or what business he had there. Whatever it was, it could wait until after Scarlett had heard what mystery had brought her running all the way back from Egypt. She made her way upstairs and knocked on the door to the lodgings.

The great detective was there waiting for her, or possibly waiting for Cruces, given what Mrs. Hudson had just said, while John Watson was standing off to one side, by the fireplace. Holmes looked as he always did, with the wiry frame of a man in his thirties, that sharp, almost beak like nose, and those piercing eyes that always seemed to see through everything they touched. Dr. Watson was only a couple of years older than Holmes, though he always struck Scarlett as the friendlier looking of the two, with that open, honest face of his and the slight roundness of an ex-

### Supernatural Devices: A Steampunk Scarlett Novel #1

military man now eating too much good food. As usual, he kept his weight off the leg he had injured ten years before.

Scarlett looked around and smiled. "Mr. Holmes."

"Oh, there isn't the need for that kind of formality, Scarlett," the detective said. "Even in front of Cruces. I have known you since you were a girl, after all."

"Sherlock, then. And you, Doctor. Is Mary not keeping you at home with her cooking?"

John Watson laughed at that. "She tries. Tonight though, Sherlock requested that I be present for your homecoming." He drew her into a brief hug that was surprisingly tight. "Welcome back to England, dear. You are looking as beautiful as ever."

Scarlett tried to take the compliment with good grace. After all, she knew she was beautiful, with an athletic figure and high cheek bones that could hardly be called anything else. Knowing it was, her mother occasionally said, one of her few faults. It was just that she generally preferred it when people noticed other things about her, like her inquiring mind, or her mastery of languages. For now though, she had simpler things to concern her.

## Kailin Gow

"You guessed when I would be back?" Scarlett asked Holmes.

"You know I receive the occasional message from friends at the ports when people I have asked them to look out for appear," Holmes said casually. "From there, it was no great thing to determine that you would almost certainly come straight here. Did Theodore and Gemma allow you to go easily?"

"Easily enough," Scarlett answered, thinking back to their parting. It had been tender enough, but her parents had been in a hurry to get back to their dig, and Scarlett had been in just as much of a hurry to get to London.

"Good. I have often sought their knowledge with items of a more… mystical sort, so it would be a shame if they did not allow their daughter the same involvement."

Scarlett could remember some of the visits. Sherlock would come around to their town house, or to the small home in the country, both of which were filled with knick knacks and objects acquired on her parents' travels. Invariably, he would have questions about their ritual significance, or what powers they were said to possess. Occasionally, he would have questions about some monster or creature of legend. As a girl, Scarlett had enjoyed those stories the most.

All of which was enough to leave Scarlett bursting with questions, but Mrs. Hudson chose that moment to enter with a tray of tea and cakes. Scarlett knew better than to argue. No one did anything but concentrate on the food when Mrs. Hudson's cooking was involved, and in any case, one didn't turn down tea. Even in Egypt, where coffee was the preferred beverage, Scarlett had stuck to it.

"And now I'm off to bed," Mrs. Hudson said, "so if you want anything else, you shall have to fetch it."

Of course, there was enough there to feed a small army, so there was little chance of that. Holmes and Watson both took cakes with their tea, moving over to the fireplace with them while they discussed something in low tones, while Scarlett ate with the hunger of someone who hadn't touched anything since lunch. From the amount there was, she surmised that Mrs. Hudson had guessed as much.

As she ate, she watched Cruces. His features were so delicate that they almost spilled over from being handsome into being beautiful. Almost. The power of the rest of him prevented that. He sat casually, almost insouciantly, his eyes on Scarlett. He had one of Mrs. Hudson's creations in front of him, but didn't make any moves towards it. Nor did he touch the tea, nursing a glass of red wine instead. That struck Scarlett as remarkably anti-social, given that no one else there was drinking the stuff.

"What sort of English gentleman does not touch tea?" Scarlett asked.

Cruces smirked. He had the most infuriating smirk, and Scarlett knew just by looking at him that he was perfectly aware of it. "The sort who prefers wine? Besides, who says I have always been an English gentleman?"

Scarlett shook her head in exasperation and finished off what there was of the food. She had grown accustomed to eating all kinds of strange things in the course of her parents' travels, but the opportunity for Mrs. Hudson's cooking wasn't one to be passed up. Once she had cleaned her own plate, she found herself looking hungrily at Cruces'. He obviously caught the glance, because he pushed it towards her with a laugh.

"You find me funny?" Scarlett demanded. She knew that she probably looked the same as all the

### Supernatural Devices: A Steampunk Scarlett Novel #1

simpering girls in London to the young man opposite her, but she certainly wasn't there for his entertainment. She was there to help solve a mystery.

"Not funny, no," Cruces replied. "Merely in need of a cake."

As wit went, it was hardly Wilde, but it was enough to remind Scarlett of her manners. "Thank you," she said, starting to attack the contents. Even that hardly counted as ladylike behavior, but one of the things Scarlett had learned with relatively wealthy parents was that such niceties could be ignored fairly easily. How else could they have spent so much time looking into hidden temples and dusty tombs?

"It is just nice to run into a young woman who does not eat like a bird," Cruces replied, sipping his wine once more.

"I learned abroad not to bother with such fashions," Scarlett said. "How many London girls spend all their time trying not to appear fat, and starving themselves into the process? Or squeeze themselves into corsetry instead."

**Kailin Gow**

"There are those who believe that it is good for the health of the internal organs," Cruces observed, but Scarlett caught the beginnings of another of those smirks at the corners of his mouth.

"I take it that is not what you believe?" Scarlett asked.

"Hardly. I like young women who are not ashamed of their beauty, like yourself, Miss Seely, and who do not hesitate to give in to their appetites."

He glanced at the half eaten cake. Which was just as well, as far as Scarlett was concerned, because her cheeks briefly flushed the color of her name.

"I do not give in to all my appetites the same way," she warned.

Cruces raised one perfect eyebrow. "Really? And there I was thinking you were without fault. Ah, the girls of

### Supernatural Devices: A Steampunk Scarlett Novel #1

England. I had hoped you were different. Far too many are so restrained. Too restrained for my liking."

"And you do not think that I am restrained?" Scarlett shot back, bristling slightly.

"As I said, I hoped. You are clearly different to most young women, if you are prepared to try to run down thieves. Tell me, if you had caught the one who took your purse, would you have beaten him until he handed it over?"

"Do you think I could not?" Scarlett countered. Perhaps if this Cruces had seen her use a little of the French *savate* on the man, he would be a little more respectful.

Cruces gave her an appraising look. "I am certain that you could do almost anything you wanted to a man."

"And I am certain that *you* are making fun of me again."

"You would prefer a serious answer then? Yes, perhaps you could fell a man. It would make you a most remarkable young woman for this age, but then, we have already established that you are nothing like some of the vacuous songbirds there are so many of in this city."

"True enough." Scarlett nodded. After all, compared to most of the young women she met when she was in London; pretty, vacant things focused solely on coming out well and attracting the attentions of the right young men, she was something else entirely. Yet she wasn't sure that she was entirely happy with Cruces' line of conversation. He seemed far too *forward* for Scarlett's tastes. And there was a word she had never thought she would find herself using. She tried for her most serious demeanor. "I would hope that I still have *some* sense of propriety."

Cruces looked at her with such intensity that for a moment, Scarlett's cheeks burned again. And this time there was no pretense that he was not watching. "Propriety is an overrated modern creation. Something created to persuade people to spend their lives feeling shame. I prefer the older standards of Greece and Rome, where if a man was interested in a woman, he would simply go up and kiss her."

Scarlett struggled for some kind of control. It was all too easy to imagine Cruces kissing her. Imagine the healthy, wine tinged redness of his lips on hers. Imagine how pleasant it would be. "Then we have read very different books on the subject," she managed. "In those *I* have read, doing such a thing to a woman of a noble family would have been an insult, even a crime. A man could end up killed for such a thing."

"That," Cruces said, "would very much depend on the woman in question, don't you think?" He held her gaze a moment longer before looking away. "I imagine you are right though. We have learned in very different places. Oh, and you should not carry that dagger of yours in your purse, Miss Secly. It is a dangerous place to keep it. There might not be someone to retrieve it for you next time."

"You went through my purse?" Scarlett demanded, shocked not simply by the thought of that but also by the thought of Cruces with his hands on the dagger her parents had given her. Had the man no concept of privacy? Honestly, Scarlett was starting to wish that she had never gone there. Except of course that would have meant giving up on the potential for adventure, and she would not do that. Instead, she summoned up her haughtiest look once more.

"You are no gentleman, sir."

Cruces smiled. "I believe I told you that before. I am so glad there is something we can agree on at last."

# Chapter 3

Scarlett had had enough. A little banter with an obviously attractive young man was one thing, but she was not going to sit there and be insulted by such an obnoxious, arrogant, foppish-

"You really do get more beautiful the angrier you get," Cruces observed.

Scarlett resisted the urge to hit him with the nearest piece of crockery only because of what Mrs. Hudson would say. "Sherlock," she said instead, "you said in your letter that you wanted my assistance in something. Can we get to that, please? It has been a long journey, and I am eager to get back to the townhouse to rest."

Especially when it meant that she could do so away from the young man opposite her. Honestly, why were the gorgeous ones always so irritating?

## Kailin Gow

"Of course, Scarlett," Holmes said. He seemed briefly amused by it all, but then, he had presumably surmised the real reason for her haste as soon as she said it. It wasn't like Scarlett could hide anything from him. Still, he was quick enough to oblige, taking a seat nearby and steepling his fingers in that way he so often did when he was thinking.

"You are aware, of course, that not all of my investigations concern the mundane?"

"Of course," Scarlett said. She had known about them since she was a child. They weren't the investigations that the good doctor wrote up for public delight. Those merely involved the least pleasant aspects of humanity. The ones involving creatures of the night would no doubt have had them running for shelter, if they had been believed. Scarlet believed them, but she had never been afraid. She took a moment to put the pieces together. "You believe my talent will be of use."

"I do," Holmes said.

Her talent. What they used to call the second sight. The simple knack for seeing things that others didn't. Scarlett had possessed it all her life, so that as a child she

### Supernatural Devices: A Steampunk Scarlett Novel #1

had been unable to understand why not everybody could see all the people that she could. These days, she was so used to it that she hardly thought of it. The living, the dead, the things so different that most of humanity filtered them out for their own protection, Scarlet didn't see much difference between them. Nine times out of ten, the things she saw were simply going about their business. Even in Egypt, the sight of the crocodiles had been far more impressive than seeing the *ka*, the birdlike spirits of the dead, flying around the pyramids.

"Not just your talent, Scarlett," Holmes reassured her. "You have a fine mind for your age, and it helps that you are a young lady. If it had been just a question of something so simple as finding another with the sight, I would have found another way to deal with the situation, rather than waiting the time it has taken for your return."

That was something. Her gift probably sounded impressive to ordinary people, but really, it was such a trivial thing. It hardly counted as much of an accomplishment when set beside the things Scarlett had mastered through her own efforts.

"So what is this situation?" Scarlett asked, wanting to hear more. It was no longer a case of just wanting to get home, away from Cruces, as quickly as possible. His presence was merely a handsome distraction now, with the prospect of a real challenge in front of her.

"A couple of weeks ago now," Sherlock explained, "a girl by the name of Cecilia went missing."

"You take cases looking for missing girls now?" Scarlett asked. Holmes normally took only those cases that interested him, quite famously having no time for the 'drudgery' of ordinary crime.

"I do when the circumstances are interesting enough," he explained.

Cruces cut in. "And besides, Miss Seely, would you not want someone looking for you if you were to go missing?"

The reproof was clearly intended to bait her once more. Scarlett wasn't sure why the young man took such a delight in testing her like that. And it didn't help that in this case, he had a point. Scarlett wouldn't like to think that, should she ever disappear, there would be nobody looking for her. She would want the greatest detective in the

### Supernatural Devices: A Steampunk Scarlett Novel #1

country, if not the world, trying to locate her. Could she deny that much to another young woman? No, clearly not.

It didn't mean she had to show Cruces that he'd gotten to her, though, so Scarlett smiled slowly instead. "Do you mean to say that you would not look for me, sir? Or do you only find lost purses?"

Cruces gave her another of those too intent looks. "Believe me, I would follow. Who could not?"

Scarlett caught the look that Sherlock gave Cruces. There was a note of warning in it. One that the younger man seemingly took heed of, because he relaxed his attention on Scarlett somewhat. Scarlett wasn't sure whether to be grateful for that or not.

"Tell me more about the girl," Scarlett said, "and about what happened."

Sherlock nodded, apparently pleased. "She is a Romany gypsy, and was a servant to a wealthy patron of the arts who collected items of mystical significance. One of those items went missing around the time that the girl went missing."

"And you assume that she took it." It still seemed to be a very simple matter. One that Holmes normally would not have interested himself in. Was that why he was passing it off to her? Was he giving her a taste of adventure with something that would never come close to stretching him, indulging a mere girl with a simple task? Even as she felt the annoyance that came with that thought, Scarlett knew that the detective did not think like that.

"I assume nothing," Sherlock said. "Remember my method. However, it seems likely."

Scarlett frowned. Perhaps in a moment, she would see where the interest lay. "What is the item?"

"It is a ring," Sherlock explained. "A double band of gold, with the word 'Thura' inscribed."

Scarlett nodded. Even most ordinarily well-educated young people would have known that one, and she had spent years alongside her parents as they translated things from much more challenging languages. "The Ancient Greek for doorway."

"Exactly. The sources I have available suggest that the ring can supposedly open doorways into other realities, making it an object of some considerable power."

That explained at least why Holmes did not leave the matter to the police, despite the apparent lack of interest

### Supernatural Devices: A Steampunk Scarlett Novel #1

in the mystery. If the item did have any true abilities, allowing some ordinary constable to handle it might be disastrous. Even an officer of more flexible thinking, like Inspector Lestrade, would have difficulty with something like this.

"Why me though?" Scarlett asked. She could not leave it any longer. "If it is simply a matter of locating a stolen item and a runaway girl, there must surely be others you could ask. I know you have informants."

"Informants and contacts with every fence, petty thief and flophouse owner in the city," Sherlock confirmed. "Yet we must tread carefully. Locating the girl is not impossible, but what then? We can hardly seize her from the streets and force her to tell us where the ring is. Even a threat of prosecution for the theft would do little, and would expose too much of what occurs in London for most people's tastes."

"Even so-" Scarlett began, but stopped herself. She was not going to ask stupid questions in front of Sherlock. Or in front of Cruces, though she was less sure why that mattered to her. "What else? I assume there is something else, or even with a situation like that, you would not have waited for me."

"The situation is a potentially complex one," Sherlock admitted, looking mildly pleased that Scarlett had guessed that much. "There are details about the night in question and my inquiries since that I will not bore you with, but which lead me to believe that there are other forces at play here."

"Supernatural ones?" Scarlett asked, then shook her head. "Obviously supernatural ones, or I would not be here."

"You have no problem with the supernatural, then?" Cruces asked.

Scarlett laughed. "Hardly. I have seen it since I was a child."

"And how do you feel about it, Miss Seely? Do you feel yourself repulsed by it? Attracted by it?"

Sherlock gave him another of those strange looks before turning back to Scarlett. "There is that feel to things," he said. "Though I cannot yet see the pattern of it."

He sounded almost happy about that, but then, that was the nature of the man. Something that could be solved with a minute's work was of no interest. Something apparently impenetrable was to be savored the way a different man might hold onto a pleasing jigsaw puzzle. Scarlett might have thought it quite a perverse quality, if she didn't have the same bubbling sense of excitement under the surface at the thought of an adventure worth having.

"So you want me to investigate this greater force for you?" she asked.

At once, Holmes' features turned severe. "No. Let me make it clear that doing so would potentially be very dangerous. John-" he nodded to Watson "-has been at pains to ensure I do not push you towards such a thing, and for one, I am inclined to agree."

Watson looked faintly embarrassed at that. "Forgive me, Miss Seely. I know Holmes rarely thinks of the danger, and I am aware that you are a resourceful young woman, but-"

"But I *am* a young woman?" Scarlett asked, trying not to be too withering. She turned her attention back to Holmes. "If not that, then what?"

"We need someone who can talk to Cecilia," Holmes explained. "And it seems more likely that she will speak to you than to us. She has a... distaste for men."

"Because of this 'patron of the arts'?" Scarlett asked.

"He did make certain advances to the girl," Holmes admitted.

"And when he tried to press them, ignoring her wishes," Scarlett guessed, "she took the ring and left." She paused. "Frankly then, I think the man deserved what he got."

"It is perhaps slightly unfortunate that you think so, Scarlett," Holmes observed, with a look towards Cruces.

It took Scarlett a moment to work out the meaning of that glance, and she cursed herself once she did. "Him?"

"You did not guess it sooner?" Holmes asked, sounding faintly disappointed. "But then, it has been a long trip. Miss Scarlett Seely, may I present Cruces, Lord Darthmoor, my client in this affair. *Your* client in this affair, since I assume that you will still wish to work on it?"

Scarlett swallowed her embarrassment just long enough to nod. She wasn't turning down the opportunity to

### Supernatural Devices: A Steampunk Scarlett Novel #1

help. Not even now, with Cruces' smile at its most annoying.

"Tell me again," he said, "how you think that the gentleman concerned got what he deserved?"

Kailin Gow

## Chapter 4

Scarlett walked beside Cruces, only too aware of how close he was as he walked her back to her parents' townhouse in Westminster. Perhaps she should not have agreed to let him walk with her, but the young aristocrat had insisted, saying that she would never get a hansom from outside Baker Street at that hour, while suggesting that the London night was not safe for a young woman walking alone. He did not mention the incident with Scarlett's purse again, but then, he did not have to.

### Supernatural Devices: A Steampunk Scarlett Novel #1

Scarlett had eventually agreed on the basis that it would allow them to discuss the details of the case further. As it happened though, Cruces had barely said a word since they had left the great detective's home.

"You aren't annoyed with me for thinking that you would try to force yourself on a serving girl are you?" Scarlett asked.

"That depends," Cruces replied. By moonlight, his features seemed even paler. "Do you still think it?"

"I think," Scarlett said after a moment's deliberation, "that you would probably be shocked if the serving girl did not throw herself at *you*."

Cruces smiled. "You believe that I am so handsome?"

"I believe you have that high an opinion of yourself," Scarlett countered.

Cruces shrugged. "It is an opinion young women generally find to be well justified."

Scarlett rolled her eyes, this was potentially going to be a long walk home. Not that she minded too much. London after dark was almost more interesting than it was during the day. Especially for someone with her sight.

## Kailin Gow

Although the supernatural was by no means confined to the darkness, there were things that came out in the night that you simply did not see by sunlight.

Scarlett amused herself by cataloguing them as she walked. There were the faint outlines of a couple of children, playing on the street in a way that living children would not have by night. There was the barely there form of a roman soldier, his sandals treading their way along the city's streets the way they presumably had for more than seventeen hundred years. To most people, they would probably have looked out of place, but Scarlett could hardly imagine not seeing them.

"It must be difficult for you," Cruces observed, "being different. Being able to see things that others cannot."

Scarlett wondered at the timing of that question, but she decided that it was simply Cruces looking for something to talk about. After all, what else would he bring up? The dismissal of Bismark over in Germany? Some other piece of trivia gleaned from the broadsheets?

"It is simply normal for me," Scarlett replied. "And as for being different, my parents have always led me to believe that is no bad thing. After all, who would want to be the same as everyone else?"

"So you would not want a normal life?" Cruces asked her, continuing to walk.

"What is normal?" Scarlett countered. "What people think of as normal today, tomorrow might be thought of as quite old fashioned."

"You think that people change so much?" Cruces shook his head. "I find that all too often, people are simply the same. They blur together in my mind." He looked at her. "With one or two exceptions, obviously."

Scarlett let that last part go. "You must be very bored with the world, then. Personally, I find that people are fascinating. There are so many things to observe about them. So many things that make them unique."

Cruces thought for a moment. "And maybe that is a greater gift than your sight. Or maybe you just have not seen as much as me yet."

Scarlett could not help laughing at that. "You speak as though you are fifty, rather than merely twenty."

"Yes, I probably do."

They walked on in silence for a little longer, heading through the West End. Here, there was far more to see, because it was not a space that went to sleep easily. The theaters that showed the works of Shaw or Wilde were open, as were the fashionable clubs around them. They weren't as old or as respected as some of those in the very heart of the city, but that just meant that they attracted a more fashionable clientele.

They weren't what Scarlett was watching, though. Instead, her sight picked out those in the crowd whom the others there didn't react to. The ones who were as unreal to most of the people there as the ghosts before would have been. There was a man dressed in a top hat and tails who moved like smoke between the assembled throng, while smaller figures, barely more than six inches high, darted around picking up dropped coins, and occasionally jostling people so that they ensured a steady supply of coins to collect.

There were also cabs lined up outside the theaters, waiting to take the watching crowds home. As Scarlett watched, a woman wreathed in shadows she was sure weren't visible to anyone else got into one. Idly, she

### Supernatural Devices: A Steampunk Scarlett Novel #1

wondered what, if anything, that meant. Just because she had possessed her gift all her life didn't mean that she necessarily understood everything about it, even though she had tried to learn everything she could on the subject. She eyed the waiting cabs again.

"I could get a hansom from here," Scarlett suggested. "I would not want to put you to further trouble, Lord Darthmoor."

Cruces spread his hands. "It is no trouble to walk with a beautiful woman, and it really is just Cruces. Besides, you still haven't asked me everything you want to know about what happened with myself and Cecilia."

Scarlett tried to force herself to focus. Cruces was right. She had a job to do, and an investigation to conduct. That meant getting as much information as possible from the young man walking with her.

"Tell me about Cecilia," she instructed.

"What do you wish to know?" Cruces asked with another infuriating smile. "Exactly how cruel I was to her? Exactly what I did to *deserve* the loss of a powerful artifact?"

## Kailin Gow

Scarlett tried not to rise to the bait. "You aren't going to let that go, are you?" Trying to be businesslike, she pressed on. "I was thinking of something more practical, like a description."

"Ah." Cruces came to a halt outside one of the theaters. "Cecilia is about your age, perhaps a little shorter than you and with dark hair that she typically leaves unbound, but occasionally covers with a scarf. I have a sketch here, if it will help."

He produced a folded piece of paper from a pocket, handing it to Scarlett. On it was a pen and watercolor work depicting the head and shoulders of a beautiful young woman. Her features were sharply defined, just a tiny fraction from being harsh, but on her they looked merely delicate. Her eyes were large, and a brown so deep they were almost black.

"Where did you get this?" Scarlett asked.

"I painted it, of course." Cruces said it like it was nothing.

"I thought people were just a blur for you."

Cruces shrugged. "I can appreciate beauty as much as the next man. More perhaps. Though I assure you that

### Supernatural Devices: A Steampunk Scarlett Novel #1

Cecilia was only too willing to be sketched. This is all just a… misunderstanding."

Scarlett looked at the sketch "A misunderstanding of the kind that occurs when you sketch beautiful young women and tell them how attractive they are. You say that you did not try to push yourself at Cecilia?"

"I did not," Cruces insisted.

"Quite the opposite, if anything?" Scarlett guessed.

Cruces hesitated, and then nodded. "It was meant to be nothing. She is beautiful, and I see no reason to be reserved when beauty is concerned. It was easy enough to convince her to sit for me for a few sketches, even a painting, and I will admit that I toyed with the idea of making a play for her affections."

"Toyed with it," Scarlett echoed. Once more, she found herself disliking Cruces intensely. What kind of man saw love as something to be treated as a game? "You toyed with the idea of using her and then casting her aside, the way your kind of wealthy man so often does. Presumably, you will now tell me that she is just a servant, and so it does not matter."

Cruces started to walk again. When he spoke again, the anger in his voice was clear. "Why should I tell you anything of the kind, when you have already made up your mind how I think? And why should I pretend to be other than I am, Miss Seely?"

Scarlett hurried to keep up. "So what happened?"

Cruces was silent until Scarlett moved up to place a hand on his arm.

"Perhaps I decided that it did matter." He did not slow down. Nor did he look at her. "And perhaps when I told Cecilia that, and told her that I would not be painting her anymore, she took it badly."

"She thought she was your muse," Scarlett guessed.

"She thought that she had some kind of claim on my affections."

"And didn't she?"

Cruces shook his head. "She was just a girl. A pretty serving girl I happened to take a fancy to enough to want to paint her. And when I told her that much, she stole from me."

Scarlett nodded. "I think I stand by my earlier comments there."

### Supernatural Devices: A Steampunk Scarlett Novel #1

"Your earlier comments?"

"That I do not blame her." Scarlet paused. "But I will find this ring of yours. Clearly, it is not something that can be permitted to stay out of the right hands."

"And are my hands the right hands?" Cruces asked, holding his out.

Scarlett stole a look down at them. They were like the rest of him. Slender, but powerful. And perfect. "I will assume so for now," Scarlett said.

She returned her attention to the streets around them, spotting a couple of brightly shining will o' the wisps in street lamps. The creatures normally preferred marshes, but the gas used in the lighting system attracted them. They were harmless, unless you were foolish enough to follow one into the dangerous places they liked to lure people.

Scarlett tried to think about the case, pushing aside thoughts of Cruces and his hands as best she could. Finding the girl would not be hard. Not with the help of Holmes' network of informants, at least. Scarlett did not know all of them, but she knew enough, and she could speak to creatures that watched everything, never leaving. Finding Cecilia would be the easy part.

She looked up then, and found that it was even easier than she had guessed. There, moving through the crowds of theater goers, her eyes fixed firmly on Scarlett and Cruces, was a girl who looked uncannily like the one in the sketch. She wore a simple but bright dress of red and yellow fabric, with a pale shawl over it, along with plenty of jewelry in the form of silver and gold hoops.

Scarlett nudged Cruces. "Isn't that-"

"Cecilia. Yes. I think we have just been very lucky."

Scarlett wasn't so sure. She was sure that it wasn't the time to frighten the girl, but she wasn't quick enough to grab Cruces' arm. He took a step forward, and it was obvious that Cecilia realized that she had been spotted, because she did something that only someone who had been spotted would do. She ran.

# CHAPTER 5

Cecilia was away into the crowd in an instant, turning and pushing her way through the theater goers in a flash of red and yellow. Cruces started to move to run her down, and Scarlett put a hand on his arm.

"You want her to talk to you, remember? How is chasing her like a frightened animal going to do anything but terrify her?"

"You have a better idea?" Cruces demanded.

Scarlett nodded. "We follow her but we don't push her too hard. With luck, she'll soon see that we don't mean her any harm."

Of course, that was easier said than done. Cecilia had burst through the crowd at speed, and for the moment at least, the only way to keep up was to run. Or at least to run as best Scarlett could, given the limitations of her dress. Still, she followed, using the flash of red and yellow ahead as a kind of beacon to guide her, while Cruces remained resolutely at her side.

He was invaluable in that first sprint, because Cecilia's flight through the crowd had stirred much of it up. London theater-goers were not, it seemed, happy to allow people to simply barge past them, and without Cruces to push them aside angrily, Scarlett did not know if she would have been able to get through. The young nobleman kept his hand clamped firmly on her wrist as they ran, presumably so that Scarlett would not be left behind. The touch of his skin on hers was almost electric, though his grip was tight enough to be almost bruising.

They followed along street after street, heading east roughly parallel with the Thames. Cecilia showed no sign of slowing down, and if anything she seemed to be getting further away as she ran.

"Cecilia," Scarlet called out after her. Shouting in the street probably wasn't something a well brought up young woman should do, but Scarlett had occasionally had to shout from one end of an archeological dig to the other, so she knew her voice was up to it. "Cecilia, please stop. You aren't going to get into any trouble."

### Supernatural Devices: A Steampunk Scarlett Novel #1

"No trouble?" Cruces muttered beside her, not pausing for so much as an instant as he did so. "After all this? She steals my ring, runs, and now leads us across half of London?"

"It isn't half of London," Scarlett shot back, though in truth, they had already gone further than she had thought they might. Cecilia, meanwhile, showed no signs of stopping in response to Scarlett's yelled request.

"Can we chase her properly yet?" Cruces demanded. "If we take a side street or two, we might just be able to cut her off before she runs all the way to Whitechapel, or even Southend."

Scarlett wanted to point out that the girl probably would not be running at all if he were not with her, and that being facetious wasn't helping anyone. Frankly though, she did not have the breath for it right then, so she simply nodded instead and pointed to a turning ahead.

Scarlett did not have a perfect knowledge of the city's back streets and alleys. She had studied maps, and quizzed those such as Holmes who knew more, but wandering around strange back streets alone was one of the few respects in which her parents did not encourage their daughter. Still the maps seemed sufficient for the time being, as Scarlett pointed them down street after street, trying to get ahead of their quarry. At one point, they clambered up a set of stairs and over the roofs of a row of homes, climbing down again on the other side in the hopes of gaining a little ground. As she climbed, Scarlett felt some of the fabric of her dress snag, and tear. She really was not dressed for a pursuit.

They kept going, stealing sideways glances down alleys to check for signs of that distinctively bright dress Cecilia wore. Twice more, they caught glimpses of her, and each one spurred the two of them to run a little faster. Finally, Cruces pressed her flat against a wall. Scarlett did not want to think what a constable would think if he saw them like that. At best, he might assume that they were up to some nefarious activity or other, and demand that they move on. At worst, he might assume that it was some kind of moonlit tryst, which would undoubtedly cause a scandal.

As if Scarlett would ever do that kind of thing with Cruces. Despite him being so infuriating, she had to admit, with him so close where his chest was pressed up against hers and her cheeks lightly brushing his strong shoulders as they waited for Cecilia's approach, that she could imagine him holding her tightly. Imagine what it would be like for him to have his lips against hers.

The sound of footsteps in the street beyond pulled Scarlett from that thought. She waited as they got closer, and Cruces did the same, the echoes of a woman's shoes bouncing off the cobbles. Finally, and with a level of unspoken agreement that slightly surprised Scarlett, they leapt out together.

"Cecilia," she began, "it's all… who are you?"

The woman in front of her wasn't Cecilia, being at least ten years older than the girl, and dressed much more conservatively. She was carrying a package bound with brown paper under one arm. "Me? Who are you, leaping out on perfectly honest people like that? Why, I've a good mind to report you both to the police, doing things like that!"

She bustled off, and Scarlett let out a breath, looking around for any sign of Cecilia.

"If she was here," Cruces said, obviously spotting the move, "she would have slipped away the moment you chose to leap out."

"The moment *I* chose to leap out?" Scarlett echoed. "I was not the one who came up with that as a plan, as I recall."

"I would not have had to, had you not insisted that we hang back," Cruces pointed out.

"Oh, so this is my fault, is it? I'm not the reason the girl ran." Scarlett paused to catch her breath. "I just hope that woman does not really report us to the police."

"She won't," Cruces said. "Not if she is here for the night market."

Scarlett looked around herself again, and cursed herself for being so stupid. Of course that was what the woman was there for. This was Covent Garden, after all. The night market was one of London's stranger sights. By day, the area played host to all the usual kinds of stall

### Supernatural Devices: A Steampunk Scarlett Novel #1

holder, the costermongers and the greengrocers, the junk sellers and the peddlers of small nothings. By night… well, it had probably started as a way for some of London's more criminal elements to sell their stolen wares, but quickly, the market had become the one place in the city where the supernatural and the ordinary interacted openly. Those supernatural creatures who can manifest themselves enough to appear human so that they could be seen by humans without Scarlett's gift set up their stalls by night, and people would buy things that they hadn't thought possible. Dangerous things, quite often.

"You think that Cecilia has gone into the market?" Scarlett asked. That Cruces would know about it was understandable enough. After all, he had to have acquired that ring of his *somewhere*.

"Even if she has, she will have gone from it," Cruces replied.

Scarlett shook her head. "We should still look."

"I think we would be better off finding a place that stocks more wine," Cruces said, and Scarlett looked at him with mild disdain. Was that all he thought about. Bad enough that he had taken it instead of tea back at Holmes' lodgings, but breaking off the search for the object of their investigation?

"We look," Scarlett insisted, leading Cruces to the entrance to the market. There was a man on the door so swathed in old clothes that Scarlett could not make out anything of him beyond eyes that were slitted like a snake's. He looked at them for a moment, but made no move to interfere as they entered the market and wandered between stalls lit almost solely by will o' the wisps.

Scarlett had not been there many times. Her parents had gone there before, following rumors that some artifact or other from abroad had shown up on the stands, and they had allowed Scarlett to accompany them to sate her curiosity, but she had not gone without them. She had not really wanted to. To most Londoners, it must have seemed a tremendously exciting experience to wander among stalls that sold anything and everything, and which were staffed by creatures far more exotic than they could imagine. Yet for Scarlett, who saw such things everywhere, it had never seemed like something particularly different.

She realized now that she had been wrong. Yes, she saw the supernatural every day, but it was never like this.

### Supernatural Devices: A Steampunk Scarlett Novel #1

Ordinarily, it was a creature or a ghost or two standing out from the throng of humans. It was something and nothing, with which she was almost never expected to interact. Here, there were short, ugly, green-skinned creatures extolling the virtues of creams and unguents, slender, almost luminous sellers of jewelry and musical instruments, and more, far more. There were stalls for so many things, it was hard to see how they could all fit into the space.

It was also hard to see how they could possibly find one young woman in the chaos of the place. Despite the hour, the market thronged with people of every shape and size conceivable, plus a few that were not. Many of them wore clothes every bit as bright as those Cecilia had been wearing, while even those who did not were usually intriguing enough to briefly distract Scarlett, despite the years she had been seeing such things. It was, in short, the one place in London where Cecilia could easily lose them.

"Clever," Scarlett said softly. "You never mentioned that Cecilia was clever, Cruces."

The aristocrat yawned. "Is she? A hunted deer will run into a thicket to make it harder to follow. It is no particular feat."

"Enough of one to lose you," Scarlett pointed out, while beside her, a man dressed all in black exhorted her to buy candles apparently infused with the spirits of the dead. Scarlett, who could see the faint wisps of smoky spirit emanating from them, moved on hurriedly.

"Enough of one to lose *us,* Miss Seely, and I am not the one who claims to be a detective here."

"Claims?" Scarlett bristled. "What is that supposed to mean?"

Cruces shook his head. "It means that it is late, and that we will not find Cecilia again tonight. Now, if you wish to go home, you have already indicated your willingness to get a cab. I believe there are those that wait to serve the market goers. I, for one, am going to get a drink."

He set out across the market, coming at last to the side of the street, where a public house spilled light and noise out into the darkness. So close to the market, Scarlett could see that it held more than the usual run of humanity, from the ghost occupying one stool near the bar to the short man in eastern silks playing cards at a table in the corner. Cruces stepped inside.

### Supernatural Devices: A Steampunk Scarlett Novel #1

"I am going to get some wine, Miss Seely. Will you join me, or do you plan to stay out there in the hopes of catching a girl who is long gone?"

## CHAPTER 6

Scarlett did not leave immediately, even though Cruces was right and there were a few cabs waiting to take people home from the market. Instead, she followed him into the public house, taking a moment to take in more of the sights and sounds there. It was a lively place, with a fiddler playing in one corner, and people talking at a volume that made it hard to hear much else. It wasn't exactly the cleanest of spots, though. Scarlett might just have come from the heat and dust of Egypt, but she had some standards.

She only stayed a moment or two longer because of the eclectic mix of people in the establishment. There were normal Londoners there, some from the slums in badly patched clothes while others had obviously come in from more affluent areas like Chelsea. There were also plenty of stranger things, figures with slightly pointed ears or odd colored eyes, a few insubstantial ghosts drifting through the mass. Off to one side, one of the short, ugly creatures from the market was arguing with a man over whether Grace was past his best on the cricket field. Even that oddity wasn't enough to hold Scarlett's attention for long. Not when there was a case to concentrate on.

She headed over to the bar, where Cruces was just paying for a glass of that red wine he loved so much. He gave Scarlett an inviting look as she approached.

"Are you sure you will not join me, Miss Seely?"

"You are really just abandoning the hunt for Cecilia?" Scarlett demanded.

Cruces shrugged. "You saw for yourself what it was like out there. What chance do you really think we have of finding her now? No, it is better just to enjoy what is left of the evening, and then try to find her tomorrow."

That would have been the plan had Scarlett not spotted Cecilia earlier, certainly. She would have gone back to the townhouse where the one or two servants kept on by her parents to run the place would have been waiting for her, gotten some sleep, and only even thought about trying to locate the girl the next day. That was then, however.

Now, with Cecilia having led them here, it seemed utterly wasteful to simply abandon the search.

"That might be how you see things," Scarlett said, "but I do not give up so easily."

"And I admire that," Cruces said, raising his glass. "Young women who do not give up too easily make life so much more interesting."

That wasn't what Scarlett had meant, and she was sure Cruces knew it. She certainly was not going to dignify the comment with an answer.

"Join me, Scarlett," Cruces said, gesturing to an empty table. "If we are going to be working together, then we really should get to know one another better, don't you think?"

Scarlett tried not to react too strongly to that, but it was not easy. Cruces just got under her skin, somehow. And he had no right to use her given name like that. What would people think? "We are not working 'together', Lord Darthmoor. I am conducting investigations on your behalf. And it is Miss Seely."

"Well then, Miss Seely," Cruces said with one of those smiles of his. "That means that I am your employer, does it not? And *as* your employer, I insist that you join me and tell me more about yourself. The barman may even be able to come up with some of that tea of yours. Though it will probably be the least alcoholic thing ever drunk in this establishment."

At letting herself be trapped like that, Scarlett used a number of words in her head that her parents almost certainly would not have approved of. She took the seat indicated by Cruces, and the barman did indeed manage to locate some tea somewhere in his premises. Scarlett did not see the need to make things easy for Cruces, however, so she sat as primly as she could and waited for him to speak rather than offering up any attempt at conversation herself.

"You know, Miss Seely," Cruces began, "you are most lovely when you are annoyed with me. Anger becomes you really quite well."

"Then I imagine that a few hours in your company will leave me fit to rival Aphrodite," Scarlett snapped back.

"You are assuming that you do not already." Cruces took a sip of his drink. "You must tell me of your adventures abroad."

## Kailin Gow

"You called me over to hear of my times following my parents around, when we could be out retrieving that ring of yours?"

"Oh, forget that for now. It is not going anywhere, and I have no doubt that you have more interesting things to say than most of the people I meet. Tell me about Egypt. It has been a long time since I have been there."

Scarlett did her best, telling Cruces of the dig her parents were on, and the sweep of the Nile. With a little prompting, she went on to mention a few of the other places she had been: Burma, Java, even the colonies in South Africa, where the memories of the war with the Boer farmers were still fresh, and everyone seemed to be obsessed with diamond mining.

"I cannot imagine that would have suited you," Cruces guessed, more perceptively than Scarlett would have given him credit for. "Politics and rocks do not strike me as interesting you too much."

"There was little adventure in it," Scarlett admitted. "Even the things my parents find… when I left, they were excited about a clock said to belong to the Egyptian sky goddess, Nut. Do you know the legend?"

### Supernatural Devices: A Steampunk Scarlett Novel #1

Cruces nodded. "Tell me anyway. It will mean hearing more of that lovely voice of yours."

Scarlett looked for signs that he was mocking her in some way, but it seemed that he was not. "They say that the year began as three hundred and sixty days until Nut, fell in love with the Egyptian god of knowledge, Thoth. The sun god Ra, who had claimed Nut as his, became angry, and cursed her never to have children on any day of the year. Thoth extended the year for her, adding five days that weren't in any of the existing months. The clock is how he is said to have done it."

"A lot to do for love," Cruces said. "Though I suppose it would be worth it."

"Really?" Scarlett asked, slightly surprised. "From your attitude to Cecilia, I would not have thought you were a man to believe in love."

Cruces put his glass down carefully. "Just because I did not fall in love as a serving girl wished, that does not mean I am incapable of forming such an attachment." He stared at Scarlett for a moment. "Quite the contrary, I assure you. Now, you have hardly touched your tea."

Scarlett was grateful for the excuse to do something other than look at Cruces. The man seemed to have none of the boundaries that well brought up young men were meant to have. It gave him an intensity that was almost like standing in the Egyptian sun again.

"When this is over, you must give me the chance to paint you, Miss Seely," Cruces said. There was a mischievous hint to his expression that probably should have warned Scarlett.

"What did you have in mind?"

"Perhaps something after the classical fashion? I am sure your form is most lovely."

Scarlett stood up abruptly. He would really insinuate that she should sit for him unclothed? Of course he would. If she had not thought the man insufferable before, this alone would have been enough.

"You go too far, sir," she said. "And I do not have to stay here to listen to it."

Cruces' eyes danced with amusement. "Are you really so easily offended, Scarlett? I thought that you were not one of the silly girls London produces."

### Supernatural Devices: A Steampunk Scarlett Novel #1

"And I thought that you were utterly without manners. It is nice to know that one of us was right. Now excuse me. I am going home."

With that, Scarlett left the pub, though she did not immediately head for the row of cabs that still waited. Instead, she stood for a moment or two, waiting. Waiting for what? For her anger to subside enough that she could think again? For Cruces to come hurrying out to apologize? The former would probably take more than a second or two, while the latter... Scarlett could no more imagine Cruces apologizing for something than she could imagine him drinking tea. He seemed to think that just because he happened to be almost unbelievably handsome, that gave him a license to treat women abysmally. Well, Scarlett was not going to be foolish enough to let herself get anywhere near him, despite the attraction she felt for him, especially when he held her.

It wasn't like she was not used to the attention of young men. She had experienced some of that while traveling with her parents and being the only blonde girl in a sea of men during an excavation. Her good friend Gordon even, whom she knew since childhood, sometimes gave her a look that appeared more than a friendly look. Cruces was definitely one of the most alluring, charming, yet straightforward men she had ever met. And she could kick herself for feeling anything towards the rake.

Because she wasn't quite ready to go home, Scarlett headed back towards the market. If she could catch some glimpse of Cecilia, then she would be able to tell Cruces exactly what a bad idea giving up the search had been. Not that she cared what he thought, of course. She made her way back through the stalls, not bothering to heed the cries of the hawkers trying to interest her in their wares.

The London mist was starting to close in a little now, trailing between the stalls, so that they seemed even more mysterious. Scarlett was not bothered by that so much as by the fact that it meant she would never be able to spot Cecilia now, even if she were still in the market. Which meant that Cruces was right. Scarlett felt her hands ball reflexively in annoyance.

There was nothing for it but to head back to the town house, so Scarlett turned and walked towards the exit once more. She would simply have to start again in the morning, bringing together such resources as she could.

### Supernatural Devices: A Steampunk Scarlett Novel #1

She wasn't going to give up, not even with a client like Cruces. She was *not* going to fail at what should be such a simple task.

Scarlett was deep enough in her thoughts that for a second or two, she did not pay attention to the woman who stepped out into her path. She merely assumed that the woman was there to buy something from one of the stalls. It was only when the woman did not move out of Scarlett's way that Scarlett paid her a little more attention.

She was old. Old in a way that suggested any number Scarlett tried to place on it would not be high enough. She wore black, in layers of clothing that might once have looked something like the mourning clothes Queen Victoria still wore for her husband, but now made her look more like a slightly battered crow. Her hair was wispy and grey where it stuck out under a simple scarf that looked a little like a darker version of the one Cecilia had been wearing.

"If you want to find the girl," she said, "follow me."

She turned and stepped back into the mists, leaving Scarlett with just a split second in which to think. Briefly, she considered fetching Cruces, but in the time it took to find him, the woman would undoubtedly be gone. Besides, Scarlett didn't see why she should include the young aristocrat in this. It was her case, not his.

Her mind made up, Scarlett hurried after the elderly woman.

Supernatural Devices: A Steampunk Scarlett Novel #1

## Chapter 7

Scarlett followed the old woman as best she could through the thickening mist, keeping pace but not quite managing to catch her up. It wasn't quite as bad as following Cecilia, because the old woman wasn't making any real effort to get away from her, but it wasn't easy, either. The woman didn't stop at any point to let Scarlett catch up properly though; nor did she give her the chance to call for Cruces. Not that Scarlett would have called for Cruces right then, of course.

Scarlett couldn't see much through the mist, but she still had a reasonable idea of where she was. Time spent finding her way around old tombs with her parents had given her a good sense of direction, and she was not going to be disoriented by a little mist.

When the old woman turned into an unlit alley, Scarlett had a moment of apprehension though. Why lead her down there, into a place that really did not look safe?

Why lead her along like this at all, rather than simply telling her where to find Cecilia? It did not make sense. Would it not make more sense, in fact, to suggest that this was all some kind of trick?

Scarlett could see how it would work all too easily. The old woman, or an accomplice, had undoubtedly overheard her speaking with Cruces about the young woman they were trying to find. They would also have seen that Scarlett and Cruces appeared to have money, and marked them out as potential victims for a robbery. All they had to do was lure Scarlett away to somewhere she could not call for help.

If she had any sense, therefore, Scarlett would turn around and walk away without setting a foot in that alley. Two things stopped her. The first was the thought that it was only an old woman. Scarlett was more than capable of protecting herself against even a strong and dangerous attacker, so one rather frail assailant would not represent much of a threat. She had not seen anyone else around, so the odds on there being more potential robbers were slim.

The second, and much more compelling, reason came with the thought of what Cruces would say if he

### Supernatural Devices: A Steampunk Scarlett Novel #1

found out that Scarlett had an opportunity to recover the ring Cecilia had taken from him, but had not gone through with it. It wasn't that he would be angry. No, it was far worse than that. He would laugh. He would laugh, or he would claim that he understood, and make it clear that Scarlett was just one more helpless young woman playing at being independent, when in fact she could not bring herself to take the smallest risk. Scarlett was not going to let him think that. Not after all his other small insults.

So Scarlett forced herself forward. She had her knife if it came to violence, and she had her wits to keep her safe from everything else. She strode forward, determined to demand an explanation from the old woman, and find out one and for all what, if anything, she knew about Cecilia's sudden flight.

The woman was waiting for her at the end of the alley. There did not seem to be anyone else there, which made Scarlett feel briefly very foolish. After all, there was no chance that such an elderly woman was going to try to rob her alone. At worst, the woman would try to fool her with vague promises of information in return for money, which Scarlett would be able to get around easily enough.

She stepped forward more confidently, advancing until she was only a pace or two from the gypsy woman.

"You are looking for the girl, Cecilia?" The woman demanded.

Scarlett nodded. "But I will warn you now. You'll get nothing from me until I see proof that you know where she is."

"Proof?" The old woman smiled for a moment, and it was not a pleasant smile. "Yes, I will give you proof. Come here."

"I am close enough," Scarlett said, still wary enough to want to keep her distance. After all, why should the woman want her any closer than she was? Whatever she had to say, she could say without them being any closer.

The woman nodded, and for a moment her eyes flashed. "Yes, you are."

She lunged forward. Scarlett moved to defend herself, but she misjudged how quickly the other woman would move. She sprang forward with the vigor and speed of a young man. A *strong* young man. When her fingers clamped around Scarlett's wrist, Scarlett thought that she could feel the bones grinding. Her other arm went around Scarlett's waist, gripping her tightly.

"You should not fight," the woman warned. "You would not want to fall."

"Fall?" Scarlett asked, but almost as soon as she did so, she had an answer. They were moving, and moving quickly. More than that, they seemed to be moving several feet above the ground, rising like a hot air balloon.

No, Scarlett realized, rising like mist. They floated impossibly above the ground like a part of the mist around them, rising until they were higher than the level of the rooftops, looking down on the streets below where people were still making their way home by the light of the street lamps. Would those people see them, or would they be swallowed by the darkness and the mist? Scarlett doubted that there would be any help from that quarter, even if they did notice.

They travelled faster then, catching the breeze as the city gave way beneath them. The journey only lasted minutes, but quickly, there were the shadowy forms of trees beneath them, and the only trees Scarlett could think of in such quantities near London were those in Epping Forest.

## Kailin Gow

Which meant they had travelled miles at speeds Scarlett found hard to comprehend.

There were lights below, and as they got closer, Scarlett saw that they were the lights of campfires. Those campfires sat in front of colorful wagons, elaborately carved and painted, with people sitting outside wearing clothes that were brightly patterned and a long way from the usual fashions of the city.

Scarlett felt her feet touch the earth, and the grip on her vanished. She stepped away, turning around to confront the woman who had stolen her away like that, but she was gone. Or at least, she was changed so dramatically that it amounted to the same thing. Where there had been an elderly unattractive woman before, there now stood a young man not much older than her.

He was very handsome. Handsome in a wild untamed way with the tanned skin of someone who had either worked outside or lived in a warmer climate than England. His hair fell in waves down past his shoulders, while his features had a quiet strength to them that reminded Scarlett briefly of Cruces. Or maybe it was just that both young men were quite exceptionally handsome.

### Supernatural Devices: A Steampunk Scarlett Novel #1

Scarlett would have judged, if pressed, that Cruces marginally had the edge on this newcomer, but it was close. Particularly since the young man in front of her had the deepest green eyes she had seen, outlined, quite unusually for a man, with the deep black of kohl.

Those eyes were the only spark of color anywhere on him. The shirt he wore was open necked and loose, as dark as the night around him. So were the pants below it, and the boots that came almost to his knees. The young man stood there quite impassively while Scarlett stared at him.

"Who are you?" she demanded. "What do you want from me? And how dare you snatch me from the street without so much as a by your leave? More to the point, how did you do it?"

There was one difference between the new young man and Cruces, at least. Cruces would have flashed a smile and come out with some answer designed to make Scarlett feel uncomfortable. This man did not answer, and his expression did not flicker. Instead, he simply pointed towards the camp.

## Kailin Gow

So this gorgeous young man was the tall, handsome, and silent type. "What?" Scarlett demanded. "What's there?"

She did not get an answer to that. Instead the young man just kept pointing. Scarlett sighed and gave up. Apparently, all she could do was go along with what her abductor wanted. Perhaps that would give her more answers. There was clearly something supernatural going on. Flying there had been something of a clue in that respect. Yet Scarlett had learned often enough that 'supernatural' was not an explanation in itself. The things that she had always seen with her gift still needed to be thought about and examined, questioned and pieced together. She just hoped that there would be answers further into the camp.

There were plenty of people in the gypsy encampment, mostly gathered about the fires. The men wore loose outfits similar to the one worn by the young man who had brought her there, though theirs were generally more colorful. The women were even brighter, dressed in layers of flamboyant cloth offset with jewelry that gleamed golden in the firelight. There were a few children about too, running among the fires even though Scarlett suspected that they should have been in bed by that time. In a wave of tiredness that probably stemmed from trying to do too much so soon after travelling across a whole continent, Scarlett knew that *she* certainly should have been.

She knew too that gypsies sometimes stopped in the forest near to London, but she wondered what had brought this particular band there. Had they been staying long, or were they simply there to take advantage of things like the market. Scarlett knew that many bands were better at trading with the things beyond the normal than most city folk, so perhaps that was it, though it did nothing to explain what she was doing there.

As Scarlett moved through the fires, she attempted to start a conversation or two with the people there. They were polite enough, but Scarlett could sense their wariness at the presence of an outsider, and she was not sure what she should ask them. All she could do was stand there and try to think. Why would the young man have brought her here?

Then she looked over to another of the fires, and saw why. Cecilia sat there, as bright as any of the women there, tending something by the flames. Scarlett briefly wondered how she had gotten there so quickly, but then laughed to herself. If *she* could get a ride out there on supernatural wings, presumably Cecilia could too.

Scarlett walked over. By that time, Cecilia had clearly seen Scarlett, but she made no move to run away or even rise. Instead, she just watched Scarlett approach, putting aside the sewing she was working on by the firelight and looking up at her with undisguised enmity.

"What are you doing here?"

## Chapter 8

Scarlett tried to decide how to answer that, and as she did so, she took a closer look at Cecilia. She was every bit as beautiful as Cruces' sketch of her, and she projected a quiet confidence that was at odds with the frightened young woman who had run from Scarlett so recently before. She sat with her red and yellow dress folded demurely beneath her, though there was something about her gaze that was less demure. It was challenging, with no give to it. Under other circumstances Scarlett might even have thought it a look of pure jealousy.

"Why were you…" Cecilia tailed off, looking to the side as though searching her head for the word. Her accent had a strong Eastern European trace to it, and she quickly called out a few words in a language Scarlett did not know.

The young man who had brought Scarlett there walked over. Cecilia smiled as he approached, and Scarlett had to admit it suited her far better than scowling. She could see why Cruces would have wanted to paint her then.

"Tavian."

Was that the young man's name? Scarlett guessed that it must be. Cecilia said a few more words in that language, Romanian, presumably, and the dark haired young man nodded.

"My sister wants to know," Tavian said, in a voice that carried almost as strong an accent, and which seemed to roll through Scarlett, "why you were following her. I would like to know that too."

Scarlett thought about pointing out that she would like to know why he had grabbed her and brought her here with no warning, and exactly why he could fly through the London mist like that, but she did not. He had brought her to Cecilia, and that was what mattered. Scarlett was not going to risk asking questions that would only make it less likely to get the answers she wanted. It would be far better to focus on what she needed to know, and leave the rest for now.

"My name is Miss Seely," she said. "Scarlett. I am here about the time Cecilia worked for Lord Darthmoor."

**Supernatural Devices: A Steampunk Scarlett Novel #1**

Scarlett looked from the girl to her brother. How much would Cecilia understand? Ordinarily, Scarlett was good with languages, but she had never had a reason to learn Romanian.

"Lord Darthmoor?" Cecilia stiffened as she repeated the words, her expression hardening once more in a way that made it clear Scarlett had said the wrong thing.

"Please," Scarlett said, looking at Tavian, "I just want to know what happened. I am not here to cause trouble for your sister."

Tavian and Cecilia spoke for a moment or two, and Cecilia stood, gesturing sharply as she spoke. Tavian translated.

"What happened is that Lord Darthmoor tried to push his attentions on my sister, and she had to leave before things went any further. She wanted no part of him."

That did not match with what Cruces had said, but it *did* match Holmes' assessment of what had happened. Right then, Scarlett could easily imagine Cruces lying to her, trying to seduce his servants, but she had to be sure.

"So you didn't feel anything for him?" Scarlett asked Cecilia, speaking to her directly. "I know he's a very handsome man. Very dashing. I know how it feels when he is near you. How it feels like you want to..."

"You?" Cecilia's eyes flashed. When she spoke again, it was in perfect English. "You think he would want *you*? Maybe he does. Maybe he prefers blonde English gentlewomen to dark haired gypsy girls."

Scarlett wondered at the ruse briefly, but only briefly. Presumably, it had been to give Cecilia an excuse not to say more than she wanted, and to keep her brother close. Right then though, Scarlett had more immediate problems. If she did not placate Cecilia quickly, she doubted that she would ever see Cruces' ring. After the last outburst, she had no doubt that Cecilia had feelings for Cruces, so being seen as the woman who had replaced her in his affections would only harm her chances. It was just as well it was not true.

"You think that Lord Darthmoor and I..." Scarlet forced herself to laugh. "Not if he were the last man on Earth."

"You don't like men with exotic looks?" Tavian interjected, with a questioning glance at Scarlett.

Wonderful. Apparently, placating one sibling would only insult the other, unless she was very careful.

"It isn't that," Scarlett said. "If anything, he is very handsome." That earned her another look of hatred from Cecilia. "It is simply that he is far too forward. Too unrestrained. The man has no sense of decorum at all."

"So he made an advance to you," Cecilia guessed, in a tone that made it clear she did not think Scarlett was worth her former employer's attention. Her brother, on the other hand, seemed faintly amused.

"Could you blame him Cecilia?" Tavian demanded. "Miss Seely is a very beautiful woman."

Scarlett squirmed with embarrassment while Cecilia took a break from staring at her with hatred to shoot the same look her brother's way. That solved one question at least. Had Cecilia truly left to try to avoid Cruces, she would not have cared about Scarlett and any relationship she believed the two had. Cecilia's jealousy fit far better with the story Cruces had told than the one Tavian had given her. Scarlett decided to press it.

"Tell me the truth, Cecilia," she said. "You wanted more from Lord Darthmoor than he was willing to give you, didn't you?"

"It was not like that," Cecilia insisted hotly. "You do not understand."

"Then help me understand," Scarlett suggested. "Why don't you start by telling me why you took his ring? Was it jealousy? A way to get back at him? Or did you simply want a keepsake of him?"

"No!"

"Really?" Scarlett asked. "So would you still have taken the ring if he had cared about you the way you wanted him to? Are you just a thief?"

Cecilia said something to her brother that Scarlett did not understand. Tavian nodded, and then took Scarlett's hand, bending low to kiss it. Scarlett found herself reminded of the gesture Cruces had used on meeting her.

"I hope, Miss Seely, that I will eventually have the chance to show you that my people are more civilized than the impression you must have formed of us."

"I never believed otherwise."

### Supernatural Devices: A Steampunk Scarlett Novel #1

"For now though, my sister wishes to speak to you in private."

"It was a pleasure meeting you," Scarlett managed to say, and in truth she suspected that it was. After all, without Tavian, she would not have found his sister. And Scarlett had to admit he was a most pleasant young man. Tavian left them then, beaming as he went, leaving Cecilia behind to look at Scarlett with suspicion. Even so, Scarlett hoped that this need for privacy meant that the other young woman might be ready to open up to her and tell her what she needed to know.

"Will you tell me more about Lord Darthmoor's ring?" Scarlett asked. "It must be very important for you to take it like that."

"It is not his ring." Cecilia sat down by the fire, folding her arms. Because it seemed that she was unlikely to get answers standing over the girl, Scarlett sat down too. After all her travelling dress had been through recently, a little dirt would not hurt it.

"He says that it is."

Cecilia shook her head sharply. "He is a liar then, and a thief. And you…"

"I am just here to find out what is going on," Scarlett promised. "What I said before is true. I really have no interest in Lord Darthmoor."

Cecilia snorted. "If that were true, why would you even be here?"

"I am here because that is what I do," Scarlett explained. "I am a detective."

"You are with the police?"

Scarlett shook her head. "No, nothing like that. But I like to investigate things, and Cruces... Lord Darthmoor, is paying me to investigate the ring."

"I thought women in London stayed inside drinking tea," Cecilia said. "Not going around investigating things."

Scarlett smiled just a little. "Sometimes we manage to do both. Although I might not get many more chances if I do not find out what happened to the ring, you understand?"

"And you will give it back to him," Cecilia said.

Scarlett considered lying, but thought better of it. Instead, she nodded. "Unless there is a good reason not to."

"There is a reason," Cecilia insisted. "The ring is not his."

### Supernatural Devices: A Steampunk Scarlett Novel #1

"It was in his collection," Scarlett pointed out, "and you took it from him."

"Just because he paid for it, that does not make it his." Cecilia looked momentarily angry again. "He is a plunderer. A thief. That ring belongs to my people. It has been ours for many years. It is the property of royalty, not of some… collector."

Scarlett had heard that argument occasionally. Some people argued that even what her parents did was wrong, because they took treasures from far off places, removing them from where they belonged. But Scarlett suspected that this was different. Not least because of the nature of the artifact involved. Could it really open doors to other realities?

"May I see the ring?" Scarlett asked.

"You will try to steal it."

Scarlett shook her head. "No. You have my word. For now, I just wish to see it."

Cecilia hesitated for a second or two, but finally, she nodded and reached into the folds of her dress. She drew out a purple velvet bag closed with a draw string that was currently tied in a complex knot.

"My knot," Cecilia explained, "so that I will know if anyone else tries to open it."

The girl sounded quite proud of the idea, though Scarlett was not sure what would stop someone from simply taking the whole bag. Still she did not voice that thought as Cecilia carefully unpicked the knots. She tipped the contents out into the center of her palm, holding her hand flat but obviously ready to snatch it back should Scarlett try to go back on her word.

In her hand sat a golden ring formed from a double braid of the metal, just as Scarlett had been told to expect. The word *Thura*, for opening, was on the inside. Why there should be Ancient Greek on something supposedly of Eastern European origin, Scarlett did not know. Was Cecilia lying? After all, it seemed to make as much sense that the ring was rightfully Cruces. He had said himself that he was not English. Could he be Greek?

Scarlett did not get chance to make that point to Cecilia, however, because at that moment, a hand clamped over her mouth. She saw the same happen to Cecilia, while at the same time, Scarlett found herself dragged to her feet. Behind her, someone started to chant in a low, sonorous

### Supernatural Devices: A Steampunk Scarlett Novel #1

tone. Scarlett tried to turn and see what was happening, but the grip on her held her fast. While the chanting... the chanting was so soothing... so very...

Scarlett found herself quite grateful in that moment for the presence of whoever was holding her. At least that way, it meant that, as she fell into sleep, she did not topple to the floor. She just collapsed into strong arms, already too deeply asleep to care why.

## CHAPTER 9

"Scarlett, wake up."

At the sound of Cruces' voice, Scarlett roused herself. It was far from easy. It felt like she was dragging herself upwards from a great depth, and it took an effort to open her eyes. When she did so, she saw that she was no longer in the gypsies' camp, but was instead in a high ceilinged building with posters on the walls advertising everything from the tailors of Saville Row to devices designed to invigorate the constitution. She also appeared to be laying on a bench. It took her a moment to place the details of the location, but when she did, she sat up to find Cruces sitting beside her.

"This is a railway station," Scarlett observed.

Cruces nodded. "Victoria Street, to be precise. You took some finding."

"How *did* you find me?" Scarlett asked.

### Supernatural Devices: A Steampunk Scarlett Novel #1

Gently, Cruces reached out to take her wrist, exposing the inside of it. There sat a small mark in the shape of a crown and an eagle. "My mark. With it, I can track you quite easily."

"You marked me?" Scarlett was not sure how to feel about that. On the one hand, it had apparently meant that Cruces could find her. On the other, she was not cattle to be branded. Certainly not without her consent. "When?"

"Last night," Cruces said. "It seemed like a necessary precaution, and I am glad I did now. I should have warned you that Cecilia has a penchant for sleeping draughts and spells."

Scarlett thought back to the chanting she had heard back in the camp. "No," she said, "that was not her. Cecilia was attacked too. There were other people there. Men, I think. They were the ones who did this."

Cruces thought for a moment. "Then you are lucky that this is all they did, and that I was able to find you so quickly."

"When did you start looking for me?" Scarlett asked. She had not thought that Cruces would care enough to bother. At least not for a day or two.

"Almost immediately after you left the public house, of course. I knew you would not let things rest."

"And yet you did not find me at the camp?" Scarlett asked.

Cruces looked faintly embarrassed. "I told you that the gypsies like to use spells. One of them wards off certain... categories of people. I could not approach."

Scarlett started to ask what category that might be, when she looked over to the side, where a news stand stood, selling the broadsheets. By it, she saw a familiar face. Tavian. The handsome young gypsy man stood there staring straight at her, and the instant Scarlett noticed him, he beckoned to her.

Scarlett stood, and Cruces stood with her. "Forgive me," she said to Cruces politely. After all, he had come after her to help her, "but it seems that there is something I must take care of. Will you excuse me a moment?"

Cruces looked past her, to where Tavian still stood. "I do not think it is a good idea for me to leave you alone right now." He waved off Scarlett's complaint. "Yes, yes, I know that you are a perfectly capable young woman, more than able to defend yourself, but I suspect this game has become much more dangerous. You remember the group Holmes mentioned, the Order?"

Scarlett nodded.

"Well, if they were involved, you are fortunate to be alive. Why exactly they left you, I do not know, but I will not take any further risks. I take it the young man is from the gypsy camp? He looks it."

"That is Tavian," Scarlett said. "Cecilia's brother. And I think he happens to look very handsome."

Cruces subjected Tavian to a brief appraisal. "I suppose if your tastes run to the wild and the unruly. Though I think you will agree that he is not quite as handsome as I am."

Scarlett laughed at that. "You have quite an opinion of yourself. Would you agree that *anyone* was as handsome as you?"

Cruces raised an eyebrow. "More to the point, would you, Scarlett?"

Scarlett let that go. It had been a long night, and even if it seemed to be morning now, she was too tired to complain about Cruces using her first name. "I still do not think you should go over there with me," she said.

"And I insist that I should, if that is Cecilia's brother."

"You know the gypsies don't like outsiders," Scarlett argued. "You have said yourself that they put up wards to keep those like you out. Do you wish to cause trouble?"

"Usually," Cruces said, "but not in this case. I will watch you from here then. Watching seems to be the eternal curse of my kind."

His kind. Another small hint for Scarlett to digest. For now though, there was the question of Tavian, who stood there looking just as dark and brooding as he had the previous night, but whose face lit up as Scarlett approached.

"Tavian?" Scarlett began. "What are you doing here?"

She did not bother asking how he had found her. After Cruces had done it so easily, it hardly seemed worth asking.

"I came to find you," Tavian said. "My sister is gone. They took her. The Order took her."

### Supernatural Devices: A Steampunk Scarlett Novel #1

He knew about the Order too. It seemed that Scarlett knew far less than everyone about what was going on. She was not sure that she liked the sensation.

"If they have taken Cecilia," Scarlett said, "it is probably because of the ring she took. She was showing it to me when she was abducted."

"Then you must help," Tavian insisted.

Scarlett spread her hands. "What can I do to help? I have already proved that I can be targeted by them as easily as anyone."

More than that, there was Holmes' warning to consider. He had explicitly instructed her to steer clear of any deeper conspiracies. Part of Scarlett, however, the part that resented being kept on the edges of things like that, pointed out to her that she would still just be looking for Cecilia and the ring.

"You are already different," Tavian explained. "Most people the Order get to… disappear, but they left you. I wonder…"

He moved close to Scarlett. So close that Scarlett could imagine what it would be like being swept up in an embrace by him. So close that she half imagined that might be what the young man had in mind. Yet what Tavian actually did was to turn Scarlett around and raise her hair. His fingers touched a tender spot on her neck, and for an instant, Scarlett was surprised by the movement, but it was so gentle, so careful, that she did not complain.

"They have marked you," Tavian said. "They have tattooed you with the symbol of the Order."

Two marks discovered in almost as many minutes. Honestly, Scarlett wondered, did nobody bother to ask before doing this kind of thing anymore? She was not quite as scandalized by the thought of tattoos as some young ladies might have been; after all, she had spent time with her parents wandering among tribes who thought of such things as entirely natural, but even so…

"For crying out loud," Cruces said from so close to her that Scarlett started once more. How had he moved so fast and so silently? Scarlett tried not to move as his fingers traced the same path over her neck that Tavian's had. "He's right. It is the mark of the Order."

"Are you going to tell me what that means then?" Scarlett demanded, turning to face Cruces and Tavian. "Or am I to be left to guess? What is this Order, and why would it mark me?" Scarlett tried not to show any of the worry that she felt. Annoyingly though, Cruces obviously picked up on it.

"Chin up, Scarlett. It's not that much to worry about."

"It is," Tavian said.

"Well yes," Cruces admitted, "it is. After all, the Order is probably the single most evil group around, dedicated, as far as I can tell, to nothing more than causing death and destruction in any world they can find, human or otherwise."

That was indeed quite a bit to worry about. Scarlett shuddered. "Just how dangerous are they?"

"Exceptionally," Cruces said. "They are deceitful things, largely supernatural, but able to appear as ordinary enough people. Worse, if they have marked you rather than taking you, it means that they have plans for you."

"Why would they want my sister?" Tavian asked. "Why would they want the ring?"

Cruces shrugged. "It is powerful, but the details... who knows? I do know that the last time the Order made a play in London, they made an almighty mess. They started a feud between vampires and-"

"And gypsies," Tavian said. "Yes, I know. At least as well as you. Now though, I must try to find my sister."

He turned to Scarlett, looking her in the eyes so that she could take in the deep green depths of his gaze. He stared just a second or two longer than he should have.

"Farewell, Miss Seely."

He hurried off, deeper into the station, and for a second or two Scarlett found herself staring after him. She tried to pretend as she did so that her heart was not beating faster. Beside her, Cruces made a small sound of disapproval.

"You know, he really isn't your type, Scarlett dear. You shouldn't let your heart start fluttering at the thought of him."

Scarlett turned to Cruces, finding him slightly closer than he should have been when she did so. "I am not your dear, and at least Tavian has manners. In fact, I shall go after him. Presumably, he did not come here to ask for my help idly, and it was he who found the mark on me after all. Whereas you just added one of your own."

### Supernatural Devices: A Steampunk Scarlett Novel #1

"True," Cruces said without so much as a trace of remorse. "Of course, he neglected to tell you that the two marks serve much the same purpose. Just as mine allowed me to find you here, the Order's will allow them to track you down any time they choose."

"Any time?" Scarlett repeated.

Cruces smiled, but there was genuine sympathy in this one. "It is a worrying prospect, is it not? The greatest bunch of killers and mischief makers out there wants to know where you are at all times. Worse, when they have gotten whatever it is they want from you, they will undoubtedly take you the way they took Cecilia."

Scarlett swallowed, forcing her expression to something approaching firmness. "You are trying to frighten me."

"Only because you should be frightened," Cruces explained.

Scarlett raised an eyebrow. "Only that?"

"Well, no," Cruces admitted. "I was also hoping that I might be able to persuade you to let me walk you home. After all, we have much to discuss."

Scarlett thought about everything that had happened to her since meeting Cruces. She thought about the marks on her, the different stories he and Cecilia had told her, and about the new threat from the Order. She also thought about the fact that she had arrived in London the previous night and had still not been home.

"Yes," she agreed at last. "I think that we do."

## Chapter 10

It was as they walked along Grosvenor Place that Scarlett realized that they were not heading in the correct direction to see her safely home. She told Cruces this, and the young man nodded.

"I said that I would walk you home, Miss Seely," he pointed out. "I did not say that it would be to *your* home."

"You mean that we are going to yours." Scarlett paused, half inclined to simply turn around and head for her own home. It was not much of a walk. Certainly not compared to the distances she had covered the previous evening. "You are taking a tremendous liberty there, Lord Darthmoor."

Cruces smiled. "I think it is not that kind of liberty you are worried about."

Scarlett drew herself up to her full height. "Exactly what are you suggesting?"

"I meant the mark on your wrist. Why, what did you *think* I was suggesting?"

They both knew exactly what Scarlett had thought in that moment. "Isn't that mark of yours bad enough? You have said yourself that the Order is evil, yet as far as I can see, you have done exactly the same thing as them."

"For very different reasons," Cruces insisted, stopping long enough to take both of Scarlett's hands. "I put my mark on you because I would not want anything to happen to you."

"And why would you care if anything happened to me?" Scarlett demanded. "You barely know me."

"Well," Cruces said lightly, "Holmes *is* a friend, and I should hate to earn his enmity. Besides, you are a most intriguing young woman. Who would I annoy if you were not around?"

Scarlett rolled her eyes. "I have a feeling that you would find someone."

"Oh, undoubtedly, but no one who could look so beautiful when annoyed." Cruces expression changed a fraction. "You are the daughter of famed archaeologists Thomas and Gemma Seely… believe me, you are a little more known than you think. Please, come with me to my home. It is as close as your own, and I would like you to see it. Besides, we should discuss the case."

Scarlett could not argue with that. Cruces was her client, after all. So she went along with him as he led the way up into Piccadilly, near to the palace and probably the most exclusive area of the city. Merely having money was not enough to obtain a house there under most circumstances. It was also necessary to know the right caliber of people, and for them to smooth the way. Cruces was obviously even wealthier than he looked.

One curiosity of Piccadilly was that the houses there did not reflect great wealth from the outside. They were not mansions, and they generally did not stand within grounds. London had too little space for that, even when it came to the very wealthy. The houses there reserved their wealth for their interiors, and expressed their status in their proximity to the queen's residence. Cruces' home was close.

## Kailin Gow

It was a townhouse in the style of all the others, with three floors making up for the lack of horizontal space. As Cruces showed Scarlett inside, Scarlett could not help noticing small statuettes, apparently made from bronze and brass, in the shape of birds, small animals, and stranger creatures. As they approached, one or two of them seemed to move, their heads turning to follow Scarlett's motions.

"Automata," Cruces explained. "Mere toys compared to some of my other experiments, but useful nonetheless."

"You are a man of science?" Scarlett asked. She found that slightly hard to believe. Cruces did not strike her as serious enough to undertake real research. Yet compared with everything else about him, it would not be so very impossible.

"Yes, would you like to see?" Cruces led the way through to what might originally have been a billiard room, though it now seemed to serve more as a laboratory or work room. An array of glass beakers occupied a workbench at one side, while books sat on shelves nearby. A microscope occupied a small bench, along with tools that looked almost like those of the jeweler's art. There were pieces of brass cut out in neat shapes there, forming the half-finished structure of a mechanical bird. Towards the ceiling of the room, there were what appeared to be small balloons, with what appeared to be designs for carriages or larger baskets beneath them.

"In just a year or two," Cruces explained, "I expect significant improvements to be made in the realm of lighter than air vehicles. Why, I would not be surprised if they came to replace the coach and horses as the dominant mode of long distance transportation."

"That seems a little far-fetched," Scarlett suggested.

"Really? But it is simply a question of finding the right gas with which to work. We live in an age of unparalleled wonders, Miss Seely, where anything is possible."

"And you are such an expert on hot air anyway."

Cruces laughed at that. "There. Most young women would not have dared to make that comment for fear of offending me. You are a wonder yourself, Miss Seely. Please, look around my work, and I will prepare tea. Then, if you are hungry, we will breakfast."

Scarlett raised an eyebrow. "I thought you were not a man for tea."

"I do not drink it much these days," Cruces admitted, "but I know enough about it to make a decent cup. I even used to own a tea plantation or two out in the East Indies and Malaya."

Cruces bustled off into another room, while Scarlett busied herself looking at his various books. Who was this fascinating young man? He used to own a tea plantation or two, had his own residence, paint, made scientific inventions, and collected artifacts. Yet he looked barely a few years older than her.

There walls of books covering all the usual sciences, plus there seemed to be a few volumes that were written by hand, in a mixture of languages. They seemed to record experiments, with detailed drawings of devices that seemed impressive in their complexity. There were designs

### Supernatural Devices: A Steampunk Scarlett Novel #1

for automata intended to help around the home, for something that appeared to be some kind of counting machine, and which had the note 'improvement on Babbage's design?' beside it, and even for a kind of spherical diving bell with small clockwork engines to allow it to maneuver beneath the waves.

"Would this work?" Scarlett asked as Cruces came back with the tea.

"Undoubtedly, with the right materials. The design would spread the pressure of the water evenly, so it is merely a question of coming up with a sufficiently strong yet clear substance. I have tried a few things. And now *you* must try your tea."

Scarlett did. It was better than she had imagined it would be. It was warm, strong, and smooth…the flavor evenly dispersed. "You said that we would talk about the case," she said after she had sipped it. "Or was that simply a ruse to get me here?"

"Not at all," Cruces said. "From what you said back in the station, you found both Cecilia and the ring immediately before the Order acted."

Scarlett nodded. "I did. I also listened to what Cecilia had to say on the subject. You know that she considers you to be a thief?"

"*I* am meant to be a thief?" Cruces asked incredulously, but his expression grew thoughtful. "Yes, it is possible that she would believe that."

"She said that the ring was rightfully the property of Romanian royalty, and that merely buying it for a collection did not make it yours."

Cruces laughed. "I suspect that the city's auction houses would argue with that view. In any case, it is rightfully mine."

"Really, you are Romanian?" Scarlett looked at him closely.

"That is perhaps not a helpful term. The country is a young one, after all. Barely ten years old."

"But you are from that region?" Scarlett pressed.

Cruces cocked his head to one side. "I notice that you do not question whether I am royalty or not."

It was Scarlett's turn to laugh. "Ah, but you have to be. It explains so much about you. Your insufferable arrogance for one thing."

### Supernatural Devices: A Steampunk Scarlett Novel #1

Cruces sat there and sipped his tea for a moment, then put it down abruptly. "There are more things I should show you," he said. "Will you come with me?"

Scarlett followed Cruces as he led the way back through the house, and then upstairs. That made her a little apprehensive, because a small part of her suspected that they were heading for Cruces' chambers, where a young woman of good breeding should never be alone with a man. Particularly a young man known to be a rake. Scarlett was willing to go along with him for now though, partly because whatever he wanted her to see was obviously important, and partly because she suspected that Cruces was not quite the mannerless man he pretended. Indeed, once she pieced together what she knew of him, she had to wonder if he was a man at all.

Cruces led the way up to a long room at the front of the house, which seemed to serve as a kind of gallery, housing a collection of artifacts of a much less mechanical bent than those below. There were portraits on the walls of individuals who seemed to share Cruces' beauty, along with flags taken from lands Scarlett did not recognize, and which might well no longer exist. A couple of ancient swords were crossed on the walls, while a series of glass cases held objects of worked gold and precious stones, from a small coronet to a medallion inscribed with a very familiar crown and eagle mark. Scarlett looked down at her wrist. The two marks were the same.

"Do you believe me yet?" Cruces asked.

"That the ring is rightfully yours?" Scarlett thought for a second or two. "You realize that a more skeptical person might say that merely buying these things does not make you royal."

"A more skeptical person, yes," Cruces agreed. "But what about you, Miss Seely? Scarlett. What do you believe about me?"

Scarlett nodded, taking a breath. "I believe you. In fact, I believe *two* things about you, Cruces."

Cruces looked at her intently. "And what might those be?"

"The first is that you are what you claim to be. The ring is yours. You are royalty, from the region now known as Romania. The second…" Scarlett steeled herself. The deduction seemed clear enough, but it would still be embarrassing should she be proven wrong. "The second is that you are what those people considered to be the most royal of royals…an extension of the first Prince. You are a vampire."

Cruces nodded, seeming genuinely surprised. "Impressive."

Scarlett shook her head. "Not very. I should have known it the moment I saw you run, or when you insisted on that 'wine' of yours, which I imagine was blood. As it was, I had to wait until you marked me and all but said you were not human. Until you had displayed a knowledge of vampires in front of Tavian."

"You do not seem bothered by the knowledge," Cruces observed. "I imagine most young women of this time would spend their time fainting if they found out such a thing."

"I am not most young women," Scarlett pointed out.

"That is true, at least." Cruces still seemed impressed, or at least intent upon her.

"And I have spent most of my life with the supernatural around me," Scarlett continued.

"So what I am really does not trouble you?" Cruces asked.

Scarlett shook her head. "If anything, what you are merely explains a few more things about you. I'll have you know, Cruces, I find supernatural men very interesting."

## Chapter 11

With what he was established, Cruces finally escorted Scarlett back home to the townhouse her family had over in Westminster. The walk was not a long one, and Scarlett was grateful to be getting back there. She had been wearing her travelling clothes for too long now, and needed to change them for something more useful.

The house was quiet when she arrived, which was somewhat surprising. All the other homes on the street had servants sweeping the doorsteps in the early morning light, yet hers did not. Nor did anyone come out to greet her. Immediately, Scarlett was on her guard, reaching down into her purse to grip the dagger within, while Cruces moved a little ahead of her once she had unlocked the door. Neither of them spoke the obvious fear, which was that the Order had attacked her home.

Cruces went inside first, stepping into the parlor. From within, Scarlett heard a familiar voice.

## Kailin Gow

"What have you done with Scarlett?"

"Gordon?" Scarlett ran into the parlor to find a neatly but plainly dressed young man of about nineteen holding a rapier leveled at Cruces' heart, so close that it had already torn his shirt. His dark blond hair was cut short, giving his otherwise ruggedly handsome features an impression of seriousness that was not helped by his current expression. "Gordon!"

As Scarlett entered the room, his features lit up with relief, while Scarlett found herself smiling. Gordon Harris was one of the things she had missed about London. Nominally her fencing tutor, he in fact assisted Scarlett in most of her more physical studies when she was in the city, and had been a good friend for years. Scarlett had not known that he would be home. In fact, she had thought that he would be away visiting family while Scarlett was on the dig with her parents.

"Gordon? What are you doing here?"

"Looking for you, of course," Gordon answered, lowering the sword. "Your parents wired me to say that you would be returning, yet when I showed up last night, you were not here. There was just your luggage. Then we had

### Supernatural Devices: A Steampunk Scarlett Novel #1

some excitement with would be burglars in the night, and… well, you can imagine that I was worried."

"Burglars?" Scarlett repeated.

"A couple of shadowy types tried the door in the early hours," Gordon explained. "I didn't get a look at their faces, but I stayed around to make sure they did not return." He nodded to the sword. "And I kept this close just in case. I'm afraid the servants are all out looking for you at the moment. We were all very worried."

"I'm perfectly fine," Scarlett said. "I cannot say the same of Lord Darthmoor's shirt, though."

"Oh, yes, sorry," Gordon said.

Scarlett introduced them. Cruces gave Gordon a frosty nod of acknowledgement. Was that simply over the misunderstanding, or something else?

"You came down to London at such short notice?" she asked Gordon.

Gordon shrugged. "I know you, Scarlett. I assumed that the only thing that could make you come back so quickly was some kind of adventure, and I didn't want you to have to do it on your own."

"Scarlett has not been alone," Cruces said, taking Scarlett's hand in his. "I have been with her the entire time."

"So you are a detective?" Gordon asked.

"Lord Darthmoor here is my client," Scarlett said. She sat down on one of the parlor's couches, and Gordon sat beside her. "His case is turning out to be quite a complicated one."

"Then perhaps I can help," Gordon suggested, with a glance over at Cruces. Was there an undercurrent of something else in the suggestion? Scarlett wasn't sure.

"This is Lord Darthmoor's case," Scarlett said. "It really isn't up to me."

Cruces shrugged. "Let the boy help. If he is intent on being here, then at least he can try to be useful by protecting you when I am not here. Although I intend to be here most of the time."

Scarlett stiffened. "I don't need to have you around me all the time."

Cruces smiled. "That is probably what Cecilia thought too, before she disappeared along with the ring."

### Supernatural Devices: A Steampunk Scarlett Novel #1

Scarlett shuddered at that, and Gordon reached out to put an arm around her, obviously mistaking it for cold. Cruces stiffened slightly at the movement, but then, he did not know that it was only Gordon. Gordon was not making any kind of romantic move. Gordon was simply Gordon.

"What's this about a ring?" Gordon asked. "And who is Cecilia?"

Scarlett did her best to explain about the missing girl and ring. "Of course," she said when she was finished, "things have become more complicated now, because it seems Cecilia was taken by a group known as the Order. Presumably, I will have to find them now to find Cecilia."

Scarlett looked over to Cruces and found that he was shaking his head. "I'm afraid not, Scarlett. I believe this case is getting too dangerous. Especially now that you have been marked by the Order."

"Marked?" Gordon's eyes widened. "What do you mean?"

Scarlett raised her hair to let Gordon see, and the young fencing instructor tutted over the symbol.

"This is…"

"Dangerous," Cruces finished for him. "It means that the Order can find Scarlett whenever they want. It is one reason that she must be guarded at all times."

"And to achieve that, you mean to throw me off the case?" Scarlett demanded. "Do you really think I will stand for that? Have you learned nothing about me?"

"Scarlett," Cruces said, "I am merely trying to…"

"I know what you are trying to do," Scarlett interrupted, then went out into the hall to fetch one of her cases. She laid it down on the parlor floor, opening it to reveal contents that had little to do with the fripperies and finery of most young women. Devices gleamed in the light coming through the window. Several of them had blades. "I will say it once more. I am not defenseless."

Cruces raised an eyebrow. "I thought there was something different about you," he said with a smile. "We share quite a bit in common besides a passion for sleuthing, don't we? What do they all do?"

Scarlett began with a set of gold-plated goggles. "These enhance my natural sight for the unseen, allowing me to see through illusions. A gift to my mother from the fey of Scotland."

### Supernatural Devices: A Steampunk Scarlett Novel #1

Next, she took out a compass, which spun until the needle pointed straight at Cruces.

"Ah ha!" Scarlett said. "It's working quite well."

Gordon got up and stood next to Scarlett, examining the compass carefully. "Why does it point to Darthmoor like that?"

"It's another supernatural device," Scarlett said. "It detects and points out supernatural beings."

"Darthmoor?" Gordon asked. "Why, what is so supernatural about him?"

Neither Scarlett nor Cruces answered that one, but Cruces did look uncomfortable. "I should go," he said. "I did not drink satisfactorily last night, and so…"

Scarlett nodded, understanding. What would it be like to live with those constant cravings? "You will not kill anyone?"

"That is not something I do now," Cruces said. "Believe me, all those I drink from are willing enough."

Scarlett could believe that.

"Now, I will go," Cruces continued. "And later, I will ask Holmes to take over this investigation."

"Please don't," Scarlett begged. "Have I not just proved to you that I have the tools to successfully conclude the matter?"

Cruces shook his head. "The Order does not play games. This is not just a matter of tracking down the ring and retrieving it from a foolish girl anymore."

"Cruces," Scarlett said, abandoning formality in an effort to get through to him. "I am going to help you whether you want me to or not. Cecilia needs my help, and so do you. I am going to retrieve that ring for you."

"Do you really think you are going to be able to keep yourself safe from the Order?"

"I have my knife," Scarlett insisted.

"In your purse where you will have no chance to get to it," Cruces countered.

Scarlett stood and took a sheath from her case, lifting her skirts high to strap it to her leg. "Then I will simply have to keep it elsewhere. Oh, don't look so shocked, Gordon. It isn't like I'm stripping off in front of the pair of you. Did you think young women did not have legs?"

### Supernatural Devices: A Steampunk Scarlett Novel #1

Gordon, who had been standing open-mouthed, swallowed. "Not like yours, I suspect."

Cruces' eyes also lingered on Scarlett, but they travelled to the dagger just as quickly. "You know that dagger is special, of course? I could feel it last night, and I can feel it now."

"I know it is special," Scarlett agreed. "My parents found it. They believe it to have been the property of one of the female pharaohs of Egypt. It is said that she used it to execute the most dangerous traitors, and that it could kill them no matter what manner of creature they were. I think you will agree that it makes me a little more dangerous than you thought."

Cruces smiled. "Oh, I always knew you were dangerous, just not in that way."

"And you will need me for this," Scarlett pointed out.

"How so?"

"If the Order marked me but left me alone, that means that my business with them is not done. And if the mark creates the connection you say it does… well, who better than I to find them?"

Gordon nodded towards Cruces. "She has a point, Lord Darthmoor."

"I know," the vampire said.

"And you must know by now what Scarlett can be like when she sets her mind to doing something."

Cruces nodded. "I know that too. Very well then. So long as you plan to stay near her, Mr. Harris?"

Gordon nodded. "Where else would a friend be?"

"A friend, yes. And now, we should say goodbye…"

Moving with unnatural speed, Cruces took Scarlett's arm. In less than a second, they were out in the hall. Cruces' fingers drifted over Scarlett's cheeks, tilting her face back so that she was looking at him from just inches away. For a moment or two, it seemed like he might kiss her, and Scarlett… right then was not sure that she would stop him.

"I should not feel so much, so quickly," Cruces said, and Scarlett could see the gleaming tips of his fangs. He was obviously hungry. Curiously, the thought did not frighten Scarlett. If anything, it excited her. Cruces was dangerous. He was not some safe young man who would dance around what he wanted. What they both wanted. She felt her blood boiling with his touch. She knew vampires have a certain allure, a certain attraction; but she have not imagined it to be this strong.

Cruces stood very still for several seconds. "If you need me, I will find you," he promised. "With my mark on you, I guarantee that. For now though, I need to feed, and I need to leave here now before I succumb to tasting you. I will see you later in the day, Scarlett."

Briefly, Scarlett thought about telling him not to go, but that was not something she could do, and they both knew it. Instead, she just stood there as Cruces left, waited until the door swung shut, and went back into the parlor to ask Gordon if, since he was the one who had sent the servants out looking for her, he would be kind enough to help assist her in making breakfast.

# Chapter 12

A quick tour of the house's kitchen revealed that there was not, in fact, anything in it that would be suitable for breakfast. With that in mind, Gordon suggested that they might go out to breakfast instead, to which Scarlett could only agree. She took the time to wash and change first, however, picking out a simple dress of dark fabric worked with silver designs along the sleeves and hem from her wardrobe.

Scarlett took Gordon's arm for the walk, proceeding with him down towards Pimlico Market, where they had often stopped in to buy food from vendors. Possibly, a well to do young lady like Scarlett might have been expected to find a small café somewhere, but Scarlett liked finding food on the move. It reminded her of the way people ate in some of the more exotic locales she had visited, though generally with less intriguing food.

### Supernatural Devices: A Steampunk Scarlett Novel #1

Gordon had a cane with him as he walked, which fit neither with the athleticism of his appearance nor with the simple pragmatism of the way he dressed. Scarlett knew from experience, however, that the stick contained a sword blade, and was presumably so that Gordon would be able to help in the event of attack. Scarlett did not think that such a thing was likely, but she still had the dagger strapped to her leg, just in case, while her other items, the goggles and the compass, were hidden away in her purse.

It was pleasant to walk with Gordon like this. There were none of the pressures that came from being around the likes of Cruces; no expectation of anything more than friendship. Scarlett and Gordon had been friends for years, and he was more like a brother to her than anything, albeit one who spent his time helping her to improve her swordplay.

Pimlico Market was nothing like the Night Market in Covent Garden had been. It was not a place where the supernatural met the ordinary. It was simply a place for farmers and other traders to sell their goods in the heart of the city. Scarlett had often browsed it in either Gordon's company or that of her mother, picking out the choicest foodstuffs as they came into London.

Today, she and Gordon stopped at a stand selling hot sausages. Hardly the most delicate of breakfasts, but it seemed like a long while since Mrs. Hudson's cooking the night before, and Scarlett devoured hers gladly. While they ate, she and Gordon talked about the progress of the dig over in Egypt when Scarlett had left, and how much longer her parents planned to be out of the country.

"You know what it can be like with them," Scarlett said. "Their work can just take off, meaning more time away without any warning. They have already had to extend the dig to deal with the clock they found."

"Do you think they will call you back once you are done here, then?" Gordon asked.

Scarlett shrugged. "Honestly, I don't know. They might, but I hope that they will not, on this occasion. I had forgotten how much I missed London."

"Really?" Gordon asked. "I would not have thought you would have had the chance to see much of it since you got back."

### Supernatural Devices: A Steampunk Scarlett Novel #1

"Some of it," Scarlett said. "Last night's adventure covered quite a bit of ground. You know, I haven't been into the Night Market alone before."

"It must have been interesting for someone with your sight," Gordon remarked. "I always wonder how much of what goes on there someone like me misses."

Scarlett smiled. "That isn't just the market though. There are ghosts enough everywhere." She nodded to where the outline of a young woman sat on the edge of a stall selling fresh vegetables, taking out her goggles and passing them to Gordon so that he could see. "You know how ordinary the supernatural is for me."

"Well, that is good to know," Gordon said, "what with your adventures."

"Is this the point where you tell me that I should be more careful, and that this isn't the business for a young woman?"

Gordon shook his head. "You know me better than that, Scarlett."

"Yes," Scarlett agreed. "You're a good friend, Gordon."

## Kailin Gow

"A good friend, yes." Gordon looked like he might say something else, but he did not get a chance, because in that moment, a figure burst from the crowd of shoppers around them, heading straight for Scarlett. It was a young man, unkempt and tattered in his appearance, with matted hair and dirt streaked features that Scarlett might have expected in parts of the East End, but not in such a wealthy district. The young man's expression was feral as he glared at Scarlett. He opened his mouth wide, hissing like a cat and revealing wickedly sharp fangs. Then, without warning, he leapt at her.

Scarlett whirled automatically, avoiding the move while dropping to one knee. It meant that the vampire's dive took it over her head, so that it rolled, coming to its feet. Several people in the surrounding crowd cried out in fear, while one or two began to call out for a constable. While they were busy doing that, Gordon lashed out at the vampire with his cane. The creature dodged back, but it gave him the opportunity to draw his blade. He lunged at the vampire, a perfect thrust in the Italian style, and skewered it, recovering elegantly into an en garde position.

### Supernatural Devices: A Steampunk Scarlett Novel #1

The vampire just ignored it, stepping forward to swing a punch at Gordon. Gordon dodged the blow barely, thrusting his sword home again, and again, it made no difference to the creature. It did, however, mean that its attention was not on Scarlett. That allowed Scarlett to reach under her skirts and draw the dagger she had there.

The vampire seemed to sense her doing it, whirling to face her while ignoring another blow from Gordon. Gordon, seeming to sense the futility of sword work, used the cane sheath of the thing instead, striking one of the vampire's knees as it tried to leap at Scarlett once more. That brought its leap short, and Scarlett managed to slash at it with the knife, opening a wound that had it screaming its anger and pain.

"Oh, you felt that one, did you?" Scarlett asked.

The vampire's answer was to swing a rapid blow at her head. Scarlett did not bother trying to parry it. She knew she would not be strong enough. Instead, she did the one thing the vampire could not have been expecting, stepping inside the blow completely, just inches from those waiting fangs of his. It would have been suicide, except that

Scarlett had the blade she held up at heart level as she did it.

She felt the knife slide home under the ribcage, and there was just time to see the vampire's eyes widen in shock before it was gone, vanished into a cloud of silvery dust. Some of it settled on Scarlett's dress, and she did her best to brush it off.

Around her, one or two people looked on with shock, but a couple muttered about how that kind of street performance was all right for other markets, but wasn't really appropriate there, while a few even applauded. Apparently, it was the only way they could explain people who vanished into thin air. Scarlett quickly put her knife away as best she could without attracting further attention, while Gordon sheathed his sword.

"Are you hurt?" he asked. Around them, the crowds went back to their shopping.

"I'm fine," Scarlett replied, "though I wish I hadn't had to kill the creature. This way, we will never know whether that vampire was working alone, or if it was under instructions from the Order. I should have found a way to question it."

### Supernatural Devices: A Steampunk Scarlett Novel #1

"You should," a voice from beside them said, and Scarlett turned as Tavian approached. The young gypsy man looked tired, as though he had not slept. "Though I think that if you had delayed, the vampire would have ended up harming you."

"Who is this?" Gordon asked, moving forward just a little.

"Tavian," Scarlett said. "How are you? How is the search for your sister going?"

Tavian shook his head. "Not well. There is no sign of her anywhere I was able to look. I asked around the camp. I thought someone might have seen something. No one had." He nodded towards Gordon. "Is this another detective, or perhaps one of Lord Darthmoor's friends?"

He said that with an obvious note of caution, not to mention a suspicious glance towards Gordon.

"Neither yet," Gordon said carefully, "but I could be both. Who are *you*?"

"Tavian is Cecilia's brother," Scarlett said hurriedly, deciding that she needed to effect proper introductions quickly if she was going to avoid difficulties between the young men.

"The girl you are trying to find?" Gordon asked.

"Exactly. Tavian, meet Gordon. Gordon and I have been friends for years, and I imagine my parents asked him to come back to London to keep me out of trouble."

"He is like a brother to you?" Tavian asked.

"Yes, exactly."

"Very well. Now, we should walk, before someone decides that what happened here was not simply entertainment, and you have to answer questions that will be difficult to answer."

Scarlett nodded. She certainly did not want attention from the police. Not because she had done anything wrong, but because that was the sort of scandal that would undoubtedly have her parents demanding she stop her involvement in the case. She, Tavian and Gordon started to move away through the market. As they did so, Tavian spoke in low tones to Scarlett.

"You should know, I was able to find out one thing about my sister."

"What is that?" Scarlett asked.

"You understand, she is still my sister, and I must do what I can to keep her safe."

### Supernatural Devices: A Steampunk Scarlett Novel #1

Scarlett nodded. "I know that."

"But I believe that she is not the innocent victim in this she appears. I looked through some of her things, trying to find out more about the ring she had taken. I... I do not believe she took it simply because she believed it should rightfully belong to our people. Maybe a little, but not completely."

Scarlett thought about questioning Tavian on that, but for now at least, the right thing to do seemed to be to wait.

"I think," Tavian said after a few seconds, "that Cecilia was paid to get the ring. I think that she was in trouble, and that she was working for someone else, along with Lord Darthmoor."

"Someone who belongs to the Order?" Scarlett guessed. It was too much of a potential coincidence otherwise.

Tavian nodded. "I think so. I cannot be sure, but who else could it be?"

Scarlett tried to think that through. If what Tavian had said turned out to be true, then was Cecilia in more or less danger? An employer would be less likely to hurt her, but then, if things were that simple, why kidnap her? It might be that the Order had decided she was no longer useful to them, in which case, Cecilia might conceivably be dead already. There was no way of knowing.

"This all keeps coming back to the same thing," Scarlett said at last. "We need to find the Order. Do you know how to do that, Tavian?"

Tavian shook his head. "People do not find the Order," he said. "It finds them."

# Chapter 13

Scarlett was not sure exactly how they should go about bringing the Order to them, but the simplest way seemed to be to ask further questions until the Order could not ignore her any longer. Neither Tavian nor Gordon seemed particularly happy with that idea when she suggested it, but they did not speak out against it openly, and that was enough for the time being.

Scarlett set off with them in tow, ostensibly browsing the shops and emporia of Central London with the two men to escort her, but actually endeavoring to remember all that she could of Holmes' network of informants. She stopped at a small bookshop to talk with the owner about what he had heard, paying sixpence more for a copy of Dante's *Divine Comedy* than it was worth, then paused in an alley to hand a penny to a street urchin, with the promise of half a crown if there was useful information from him later. She talked to newspaper vendors and cab drivers, wandering traders and a few more specialized individuals, including one purveyor of 'artifacts' whose wares were nowhere near genuine, but who could still be relied upon to hear news in that field from those who dabbled in it.

It was not easy. Holmes would no doubt have had the information from his network over the course of an hour or so, but he had a reputation to play on, as well as access to far more individuals who might have heard something than Scarlett did. Scarlett only knew of a few of the more important informants, and they were generally less willing to deal with a young woman than they were the city's most famous detective. Money eased the way a little, but still, Scarlett got the feeling that people were not being as forthcoming as they might be.

The presence of Gordon and Tavian helped at first. Scarlett would have liked to believe that she would have gotten through all the informants without giving up even had she been alone, but the presence of two handsome young men to escort her certainly made things a little easier.

### Supernatural Devices: A Steampunk Scarlett Novel #1

They even helped to get information from some of those the three met. Those who could not believe that a mere girl might be playing at the serious business of detection were prepared to address such answers as they had to the other two. To their credit, both young men consistently reminded people that it was Scarlett they should be talking to, but she had no doubt that they got more answers than she did.

Not that there seemed to be many answers to be had. Almost no one would admit to having heard of the Order. The few that did admit they did so in hushed tones, and were able to tell Scarlett no more than Tavian had before. Scarlett tried to console herself with the thought that gaining information was not the point of the exercise so much as catching the Order's attention, but even so, it was disheartening.

Perhaps that was partly to blame for the increasing fractiousness between the two young men, although Scarlett had to admit that they hardly started the day as the greatest of friends. They were not openly hostile, but neither went out of his way to be friendly to the other, and both seemed a little too willing to pass pointed comments.

When they met a couple of urchins who were clearly looking for pockets to pick, Gordon actually remarked that Tavian should deal with them, since they were as unkempt as most gypsies, while Tavian shot back that at least, unlike most well to do young men, he knew that children like this existed.

That wasn't the worst though. Once they had been to see the bookseller, Gordon suggested that they should call it a day.

"Are you getting tired?" Tavian asked, with obviously false concern.

"No, I just do not think that this is getting us anywhere."

"Typical," Tavian said, "the moment things get a little difficult, the fop wants to quit."

Gordon glowered at that. "I am only a fop in comparison to you. Frankly, that could apply to almost anyone who isn't one of your band."

"Gypsies aren't good enough for you, then?" Tavian demanded. "Still, what should I expect from some gadjo who clearly thinks my people should not be allowed near his precious city?"

### Supernatural Devices: A Steampunk Scarlett Novel #1

"Gadjo?" Gordon bridled. "Is that some sort of insult?"

"Only when applied to the likes of you," Tavian said.

Scarlett decided to intervene. "It means outsider in the Romany tongue, Gordon."

"Well I'm glad of that, at least," Gordon said, with another glare at Tavian. "Or did you think that any *civilized* man would want to be anything like you?"

Tavian looked at Gordon, and then at Scarlett. "I think there's at least one respect in which you would love to be like me, isn't there?"

"I don't know what you are talking about," Gordon snapped back. "Who do you think you are, anyway, talking to me like this?"

Tavian shrugged. "I'll talk to you any way I please."

For a moment, Scarlett saw Gordon's hands tighten into fists. She moved quickly, stepping between the two of them.

"That's enough, both of you. What do you think you are doing?"

## Kailin Gow

"You heard him," Gordon said. "He…"

"Enough," Scarlett repeated. "You have been bickering for half the day, and I do not know why, but I have had enough. I am going to continue this trip out alone, thank you very much, and when I get back home, I hope you will both be able to behave better than this."

Scarlett walked away, hoping that her rebuke would do the trick. Because she had run through the small store of informants and potential sources of information she knew about, she headed for a nearby shop instead. Scarlett was not particularly thinking of buying anything; it was simply the best way of getting away from the two boys for a while.

The shop in question was a jeweler's, with everything from pocket watches to diamond broaches in the window. Scarlett went inside, with half an idea of asking the owner to keep an eye out for the ring, but she gave that up quickly enough. After all, the Order was not likely to try to sell it. Instead, she merely looked at the items on display.

One caught her eye almost immediately. It was a pendant necklace in an elegant clockwork design with a sapphire as the central stone, set within a web-like net of intertwining silver and gold gears, on a silver chain. Even

### Supernatural Devices: A Steampunk Scarlett Novel #1

in its case, it glittered with cool beauty, and the craftsmanship involved was quite extraordinary.

"Does that piece interest you?" A hand touched Scarlett's elbow and she turned, finding herself looking at a man who appeared to be in his twenties. He had flowing blond hair, powerfully handsome features, a complexion so pale that it seemed like he had never been out in the sun, and deep blue eyes that seemed to bore into her. There was something dangerous in those eyes too, something that forced Scarlett to fight to avoid stepping back. So soon after working out what Cruces was, and so soon after fighting another of his kind, Scarlett had no problems identifying the vampire for what he was.

"I am Rothschild," the vampire said. "Welcome to my little emporium. Would you like to try the pendant on? I believe it would suit you."

"It is lovely," Scarlett agreed, though she had not intended to spend the kind of money today that such a thing would undoubtedly cost. Before she could say so, however, Rothschild had the pendant out of its case, holding it up.

"Allow me," he said, moving Scarlett's hair aside so that he could fasten the pendant behind her neck. He paused like that a little longer than was strictly necessary, and Scarlett wondered if it was wise to let a vampire stand behind her so close for so long. What if he bite her? What if this was all a ruse of some kind? Except that even as she thought it, a second explanation occurred to Scarlett. Placed as he was, Rothschild would be easily able to see the mark on her neck.

"There," Rothschild said, "it is perfect. The same color as your eyes. Look."

He indicated a mirror off to one side, and Scarlett looked at herself in it. The pendant shone against the dark backing of her dress, and was indeed bright enough to draw attention to her eyes. It was the kind of thing Scarlett was prepared to admit she would have loved to own, but there seemed to be no way she would be able to meet the price for it with the money she had to hand. Still, she could ask.

"How much is it?"

Rothschild shook his head. "For you, Miss…"

"Seely."

"A beautiful name. And a beautiful young woman to wear it. Consider the piece a gift."

### Supernatural Devices: A Steampunk Scarlett Novel #1

"I couldn't possibly accept something as valuable as…"

"What is money beside beauty?" Rothschild argued. "The most beautiful women deserve to be dressed in the finest jewels. Besides, everyone who sees you wearing it will want to know where you got it. It will earn me far more about such a lovely neck than languishing in a case."

He leaned close to her, and Scarlett readied herself to step back. Merely giving her a gift did not give him the right to bite her. As suddenly as he had leaned in though, Rothschild pulled back.

"Roses, chocolate, and just a hint of wine. Even your scent is lovely."

"Thank you," Scarlett said automatically. "I… I have to get back to my friends."

"Then of course you must go," Rothschild said, holding her gaze for a second or two with those deep blue eyes of his. "We should not keep you from them. I am sure we will see one another again soon enough, in any case."

"Yes," Scarlett replied. "I am sure we shall."

She wasn't sure why she said that. Did she not have enough good looking men clustering around her without adding to the list? And wasn't one vampire, in the form of Cruces, more than enough? Encouraging young men like that certainly wasn't something her parents would have approved of.

Yet Scarlett knew that things were rarely so simple. She had seen other young women of her age, and for all that they might try to hide it for the sake of propriety, they felt everything that Scarlett felt when it came to young men. Scarlett was not going to pretend that she felt nothing when she was the object of the attentions of handsome young men. Nor was she going to try to put space between herself and them for the sake of how things looked, not when that would mean abandoning the investigation she had committed herself to.

No, she would keep going. She would continue as she was to see where it led. And if it happened to lead places that involved her being surrounded by such good looking men as Cruces, Tavian, and now Rothschild… well, Scarlett thought to herself with a slight smile, that was all the better.

Supernatural Devices: A Steampunk Scarlett Novel #1

## CHAPTER 14

Scarlett left the jeweler's quite quickly after that. She did not want the complications that remaining there might have brought. Instead, she went back to where she had left Gordon and Tavian, hoping that, despite her talk of seeing them once she got back home, they might still be around.

In fact, she found them in a nearby public house, drinking together at a corner table. It was a distinct improvement on their arguing with one another, though Scarlett suspected that it was not something that had come about without outside intervention. After all, Cruces sat there with them, drinking from a wine goblet. Would he be drinking blood? Scarlet dismissed the idea. An ordinary public house would not stock it, surely.

Cruces looked up as Scarlett approached. "Ah, you have found us. Were the young men so very tiresome?"

He asked that with a smirk, obviously knowing the answer.

"And you just happened to find them?" Scarlett asked.

Cruces shrugged. "I came looking for you at your home. I simply happened to run into Gordon and Tavian here along the way."

Of course he had. And his route to her home had just happened to involve this drinking establishment. Or had the two other young men simply been arguing loudly enough to be impossible to miss by that point?

"Has Tavian told you his thoughts on Cecilia?" Scarlett asked, taking the remaining seat at the table.

Cruces looked from Scarlett to Tavian, then back again. "What thoughts would those be? Does our gypsy friend know more about his sister than we do?"

Scarlett looked over at Tavian, and Tavian nodded. "He told me that Cecilia was probably working for someone else even before she took the ring. That she probably took it for the Order."

"Well," Cruces said, "we already suspected that, didn't we? Or at least, we knew that they would want it."

### Supernatural Devices: A Steampunk Scarlett Novel #1

"But doesn't this mean that Cecilia is safer than she would otherwise be?" Scarlett argued. "I cannot imagine that the Order would harm one of their own."

"Can you not?" Cruces asked. His expression grew serious. "Then I would suggest that for all you know of the world, Miss Seely, you still do not know enough about evil."

"And you do, of course," Tavian observed.

Cruces fixed him with a stare for a moment or two. "More than I would like to. I see it in the mirror each morning, for one thing."

"And there I was, thinking that your kind did not favor mirrors."

Cruces ignored that, returning his attention to Scarlett. "The truth is that some of those in the Order might kill Cecilia simply because they have no more use for her. And if she were ever to do otherwise than they had planned, they would certainly harm her. They do not tolerate those who betray them, to any degree."

Scarlett thought about Cecilia keeping hold of the ring for so long after it went missing. About her willingness to talk to Scarlett. Would those count as betrayals?

Certainly, the way Cecilia had been taken suggested that whoever had employed her was not happy with her. A thought came to Scarlett.

"Was Cecilia marked, the way I am?"

Cruces spread his hands. "I would not know. I never got close enough to examine her, no matter what Cecilia may have wanted."

"Careful," Tavian warned.

Cruces laughed. "Oh, I wouldn't want to start being careful after all these years. But you have reminded me, Scarlett. Part of the reason I came looking for you was that something felt strange. May I?"

He reached out to take Scarlett's hand, turning it gently so that the inside of her wrist was visible to all four of them. Cruces' mark should have been there, a clear impression against the paleness of her flesh, but it was gone. Just gone, as if it had never been there.

"How is that possible?" Scarlett asked. The mark had not been painted on. It had been real, and solid, and apparently permanent.

Cruces did not answer immediately. Instead, he stood, lifting Scarlett's hair with a light, sensual touch. His

### Supernatural Devices: A Steampunk Scarlett Novel #1

finger traced over the back of her neck, sending a brief shiver of pleasure down Scarlett's spine where it contacted with her skin. She wondered if Cruces knew his touch had that effect, and then smiled to herself. Of course he did.

Cruces was not smiling a moment later, however, when he sat back down next to her.

"My mark is gone, but the mark of the Order… there is a new circle of dark ink around it. A reinforcement."

"What does that mean?" Scarlett asked.

"That they have laid an even stronger claim on you. Where were you just now, when I felt the change?"

"You felt it when I was away from Gordon and Tavian?" Scarlett asked. "Then it must have happened when I was in the jeweler's. Well, it was more of a curiosity shop, really."

Cruces' brow furrowed. "Where was this?"

"Just a little way away," Scarlett explained. "You must have passed it on the way."

Cruces appeared, if anything, even more puzzled. "I do not recall seeing such a place."

"Truly?" Scarlett tried to describe it as best she could. "It was only a small place, but I noticed it easily enough. Some of the items on display were very impressive. And I recall thinking of you at the time, because it was actually run by a vampire."

"And you did not think that odd?" Gordon added from the side.

"Gordon, it is me. You know the things I see."

Cruces was silent for several seconds. "Tell me about the vampire," he said at last, in a tone that did not leave much room for argument.

"Well," Scarlett began, "he gave his name as Rothschild…"

"Rothschild!" Cruces swore, and stood so sharply that he nearly knocked over the table. "Of course it would be him. Who else? And of course he could do it. His talent has always been to get any woman he wants to desire him instantly."

Scarlett did not like that Cruces took it for granted that she had been attracted to the other vampire. He made it sound like she was some common girl with no sense of propriety. Of course, there wasn't much point in arguing,

### Supernatural Devices: A Steampunk Scarlett Novel #1

given that she had been every bit as attracted as Cruces implied, but still…

"So he was the one who removed my mark," Cruces said, looking furious.

"And who augmented the Order's mark," Scarlett reminded him. "Which means he must have something to do with them. This is about more than just your mark on me."

Cruces looked like he was having to work hard not to say something at that point.

"So what would he want with me?" Scarlett asked.

"Beyond the obvious?" Cruces demanded, making Scarlett raise an eyebrow delicately. "Rothschild is dangerous. He is the head of a group of vampires I suspect of being some of the worst criminals in the city."

"Which makes it logical that they would be bound up with the Order," Tavian interjected.

"Exactly," Cruces said.

Scarlett shook her head. "That still does not explain the business with the marks. Why should this Rothschild want to mark me? And what is this business of augmenting the Order's mark?"

"That makes the mark stronger," Cruces said. "Harder to remove. In this case, it also makes the mark personal. It is not just the mark of the Order, but a direct connection to Rothschild. It is his way of saying that whatever connection the Order has to you, it must go through him."

"And why would he do that?" Scarlett demanded. "Why would *he* care about following me?"

Cruces looked away for a moment. "It might just be to insult me," he said. "A statement to go along with the removal of my mark. Alternatively, it might be that Rothschild has an interest in the ring, and wants to lay enough of a claim to you that he is the first to learn about it."

"Or it could just be that he desires her," Tavian added, with a pointed look at Cruces, "and wants to make a claim upon her. That is what vampires do, after all."

"What would you know of it?" Cruces demanded.

Tavian looked at Scarlett. "More than enough. Tell me, Lord Darthmoor, does it bother you more that Scarlett here is in danger from one of the most powerful vampires in any of the surrounding counties, or that she no longer bears *your* mark?"

Cruces looked like he might lash out at the gypsy man then, but Scarlett stood, putting herself in the way. She placed a hand lightly on Cruces' chest, her fingers spread.

"Is that what vampire marks are?" Scarlett asked him, looking into his eyes. "Are they a way to mark… territory, for want of a better word?"

"That is one way to put it," Cruces admitted. "The signs are meant to keep those claimed by one vampire safe from others. What Rothschild did to you, what the Order did to you, it is an insult of the highest order."

"And when would you put a mark on someone?" Scarlett asked softly. "I take it that you did not mark Cecilia, yet she was your servant."

Cruces shook his head. "That is not what the mark is. It is not some nobleman's coat of arms, to be given out freely. It is used only with those closest to us; friends, confidantes. Potential lovers." There was a trace of his old smile as he said that.

"And which of those categories do you see me in?" Scarlett demanded in her primmest tone.

Cruces answered her simply, by kissing her. Scarlett had not been prepared for that. Men did not kiss women out in public like this. They simply did not. Except that Cruces did. He kissed her with an initial wave of fierce passion, which became something more gentle as Scarlett kissed him back. She knew that she should not, but she did. She kissed him back for long seconds, her lips moving on Cruces', her eyes drifting closed to feel the pleasure of it better. Cruces made no move to hold her to him though. It was as though he wanted to be clear that Scarlett was doing this as much as he was. It was Cruces' way of telling Scarlett, she was very much part of wanting this kiss as he was. Scarlett finally pulled back.

"I hope that provides your answer," Cruces said.

"You had no right to do that," Scarlett replied, though she did it softly.

"And yet you did not pull back sooner."

Well no. It had been a good kiss. A very good kiss. But then, what had Scarlett expected from someone like Cruces? "If that is what having your mark means," Scarlett managed to say, "I am almost glad I no longer have it."

Cruces snorted. "Liar."

**Supernatural Devices: A Steampunk Scarlett Novel #1**

Scarlett flushed slightly as she looked away.

"I have to go," Cruces declared then.

"You're leaving?"

"Only to find Rothschild. You don't think I'm going to let him leave his mark on you now, do you?"

## CHAPTER 15

Cruces hurried off, leaving Scarlett alone with Gordon and Tavian. She sat down heavily, aware that she had just kissed another young man in front of them, not to mention in front of all the other patrons of the establishment. It was the kind of thing that would no doubt scandalize her parents should news of it get back to them.

For now though, there was the question of where Cruces had gone to consider. Scarlett was glad of the space with the confusing mess of emotions that the kiss had brought up still swirling through her. Still, Scarlett hoped that he would not do anything foolish, even though he remained an impossible man in every way. She did not think that Cruces was the type to go out and confront Rothschild directly, but she could not be certain. She just had to hope that all would be well.

**Supernatural Devices: A Steampunk Scarlett Novel #1**

"Are you all right?" Gordon asked.

Scarlett nodded.

"I cannot believe that Lord Darthmoor would take a liberty like that with you," he said. "Why, I have a good mind to…"

"Not that good a mind," Tavian added from the side, "if you think that Scarlett here had any difficulty with it."

"Take that back at once," Gordon insisted. "You are impugning the honor of a fine young woman of far better breeding than yourself, and…"

"And my point stands," Tavian said. "Or can you not tell when a woman is kissing a man back?"

Gordon stood, and Scarlett got the feeling that he was getting ready to fight. Scarlett shook her head.

"Gordon, if you are going to be like this, perhaps it is better if you leave for now."

"Leave? You want me to leave you alone with this…"

"Please, Gordon. I think we are all a little overwrought at the moment, don't you?"

"I am not overwrought." Gordon put his hands down on the table. The knuckles were white. "But I am meant to be here to protect you."

Scarlett shook her head. "You cannot protect me constantly, Gordon, and I do not need you to. You should go back to the house and take a rest. We will undoubtedly have more to do later."

"But you will not be coming too?" Gordon asked. His eyes flicked over to Tavian, and their expression was not friendly. It seemed that the presence of Cruces had been the only thing keeping that unfriendliness at bay. How was it that the presence of such an arrogant, insufferable man could do that, even if he was quite gloriously handsome? Scarlett replayed that thought to herself, and shook her head.

"No, Gordon, I will not be coming. I appreciate your presence in London, but I do not need you at my side every hour of the day."

"That is not what your parents seemed to think when they wired for me to return here," Gordon pointed out. "How would I answer them if something were to happen to you while I was elsewhere? They would blame me, Scarlett, and they would be right."

"No," Scarlett insisted, reaching out to touch the nearest of his hands, just lightly. "They would not be right in doing that. More than that, nothing is going to happen to me. It might happen to you though, Gordon."

"I think I can protect myself," Gordon said.

Scarlett nodded. "Ordinarily. Against the supernatural, though? You cannot see it, Gordon. You cannot fight it. Not the way Cruces can. Not even the way Tavian here can. I would hate for anything to happen to you simply because you were trying to protect me."

"How does that make you any safer?" Gordon argued.

"I have both Cruces and Tavian trying to keep me safe," Scarlett countered. "In any case, I have to do this. I still have to demonstrate to Holmes that I am capable of dealing with this case, and if that means danger, then so be it. I really do think that you should go back to the house though."

Gordon looked like he wanted to argue, but he did not. "I know how important this is to you," he said, "and you know where I will be if you need my help."

He left, leaving Scarlett alone with Tavian. Scarlett sat there with the young gypsy man in silence for almost a minute before she spoke.

"If we are to find Cecilia, there are more things I should know about you, her, and your people."

Tavian spread his hands. "Anything you wish to know, I will tell. I don't have any secrets."

"Even though I am *Gadjo*?" Scarlett asked. She tried to recall the little that she had read of gypsy troupes.

"Ah, well, there are outsiders and outsiders."

"Are there? Would the elders of your family agree with that?"

Tavian smiled. "That is between me and them. In any case, Cecilia and I are hardly typical *Roma*."

Scarlett nodded, that was easy to believe. "I take it that the ability to ride the mist and change your shape aren't typical either?"

Tavian laughed at that. "Did you think they were?"

**Supernatural Devices: A Steampunk Scarlett Novel #1**

"It's hard to know what to think, when it comes to gypsies," Scarlett said. "I know that most of what people write is wrong, but I also know they have more of a connection to the supernatural than most."

"That's just what comes from living on the edges of things," Tavian replied. "We cannot ignore the truth of what is around us, because we cannot surround ourselves with cities. We cannot blind ourselves to what is really there."

"Do you think I do that?" Scarlett asked.

Tavian thought for a moment, and then shook his head. "No, I do not."

"So you'll forgive me if I do not let you dodge the question of whether you and Cecilia are special quite as easily as that?"

That got another smile from the young gypsy man. "Yes, I think I can forgive that. And yes, both Cecilia and I are different, even among the *Roma*. A few people there might have minor talents, but the things we can do are different. Tell me, is it just my sister and I you are interested in, Miss Seely, or the whole of my people?"

Scarlett thought. Obviously, she wanted to know as much as possible about Tavian and Cecilia to help with the business of the ring, but truthfully, she wanted to know as much as possible about all his people. She would not have been her parents' daughter had she felt otherwise. After all, how many times had they taken her to parts of the world that seemed impossibly exotic, and taught Scarlett about peoples there who were very different from anything she could have imagined?

"I think that I would like to know whatever you are willing to tell me," Scarlett said at last.

Tavian drummed his fingers on the tabletop. "Well, that is potentially a lot, but I do not think we should go through it all now."

"No?" Scarlett could not keep the disappointment out of her voice.

"Well, we have nothing to do but wait for now when it comes to the case, so why not join me over at the camp tonight for dinner?" Tavian suggested. "I will tell you anything you want to know then."

"You want me to have dinner with you?" Scarlett asked. "You did just see me kiss Cruces, right?"

### Supernatural Devices: A Steampunk Scarlett Novel #1

"I saw you kissed by him and swept up in the moment. I see you on the edge of feeling something for the arrogant little lord. I would like to see you for dinner tonight, so that you know that you have more than one choice here."

"You sound very certain that I am attracted to you," Scarlett said.

Tavian looked at her from under that wonderfully dark, flowing hair. "Tell me that I am wrong."

"You are very direct today," Scarlett pointed out, trying to find time in which to think. "When we first met, you didn't even speak."

"You seem to prefer directness. Please, agree to come to the camp. You will not regret it, and you will get your answers."

Scarlett bit her lip. She knew that she probably should not, but she had been there before, after all, and she also remembered reading somewhere that, no matter what people in towns might sometimes think, the Romany took the virtue of young women very seriously indeed. Dinner would *just* be dinner unless Scarlett said otherwise.

"Won't you give me at least some answers now?" Scarlett asked.

Tavian licked his lips. "I will trade you," he said. "An answer for an answer. You ask your question, but I get to ask one of you in return."

"And that question will be?"

Tavian shrugged. "Anything I choose. And the answer must be truthful. That is how the game works."

"So you are playing games with me now?" Scarlett demanded.

Tavian shook his head at that. "I might be, but in this case, it is because I want to know more about you. Will you agree?"

Scarlett barely hesitated. "All right. Why can you walk through the mist?"

Tavian grinned. "That's an easy one. Because I am not wholly *Roma.*"

"Then what-"

Tavian put a finger to Scarlett's lips. "It is my turn. Why did Sherlock Holmes bring you in to try to find the ring?"

### Supernatural Devices: A Steampunk Scarlett Novel #1

Scarlett bit back the urge to tell Tavian a half-truth like the one he had just told her. "Because I have the talent for seeing the supernatural. I have always had it, ever since I was a girl."

"Really? Then..."

It was Scarlett's turn to put her fingers to *his* lips. "My question. If you are not a gypsy, then what are you? Another vampire?"

Tavian shook his head. "No, not that. Never that. Does seeing the supernatural bother you?"

"No," Scarlett said. "It is a privilege, even if it is one I do not understand. I have the opportunity to see things that other people will never see, and that sometimes lets me help them when other people cannot. Some of the supernatural is strange, but so much more of it is beautiful."

Tavian nodded.

"Exactly what are you?" Scarlett asked.

Tavian smiled. "I could dodge that too, you know, if I wanted. But I won't. Will you stand up a moment, Scarlett?"

Scarlett stood, unsure of what it had to do with getting an answer to her question, but willing to trust

Tavian enough to go along with it. Tavian stood too, looking into her eyes for a long moment.

"It is easier to show you what I am than to tell you," he said, "and anyway, I have wanted to do this since I saw you. Especially since the vampire has already come close to making up your mind."

That should probably have warned Scarlett what was coming next. With a delicacy that surprised her, Tavian slid his hands to the back of Scarlett's head and kissed her.

## CHAPTER 16

The kiss was different to the way Cruces' had been so soon before. It was gentler, softer, and more open. It did not demand that Scarlett kiss Tavian back. It asked, and she did. Oh, she did. If that had been all there was to it, it would have been enough, but it wasn't. Instead, from almost the moment their lips met, Scarlett found her head filling with images. It should not have been possible, but she could see them clearly, could almost feel them.

She was standing on the edge of a village. It was not a large village, and it did not have a railway line running to it. It was tiny and sleepy, hidden in the shadow of the woodlands around. It was a place of tiny cottages and small dreams. And on the edge of the village, there sat caravans, where gypsies had come to ply their trades for a brief time. The scene before Scarlett shifted then, and she found herself in one of those caravans. There was a crib in that room, a rough, wooden thing containing two babies that looked to be no more than days old. They were sleeping close to one another.

They even slept when hands lifted them from the crib, placing two more babies down where they had lain, swaddled in blankets against the cold of the night. For a moment, Scarlett was not certain about what had happened. She went over to the crib bending over it to stare down at the tiny forms within. Delicately, careful not to disturb them, she peeled back the swaddling blankets so that she could see the babies better.

Both had black hair and one had familiar, *very* familiar, green eyes. Both looked up at Scarlett, making her wonder exactly how that could happen. This was a dream, after all. A vision of the past. Yet there was no doubt that even as Scarlett looked at the children, they looked back at her. There was one more surprise beneath the swaddling cloth too. The children now in the crib had wings.

They were small wings, delicate wings, like those of a dragonfly fluttering above a summer pond. They flexed as the children below stared up at her, and Scarlett had to wonder just what these children were. What kind of

### Supernatural Devices: A Steampunk Scarlett Novel #1

children had wings? What kind of children replaced others in their crib?

The answer to both questions came to Scarlett in a rush. The children in the crib now certainly were not human, because human children did not have wings. That meant that they had to be some form of supernatural creature, and one form of supernatural creature was notable for stealing children. The fey. The children in the crib were changelings, fey children left to be brought up by humans. And, since Tavian was the one showing her this vision, and since the deep green of those eyes was so very familiar, that meant…

Tavian and Cecilia were fey children. They were changelings. It was the only answer that made any sense.

Even as Scarlett decided that, Tavian pulled away from her enough to look her carefully in the eyes. His finger traced the contours of her face in a way that seemed to come half from affection and half from worry. He seemed almost afraid. Afraid that Scarlett would recoil from what she had just seen, perhaps?

"Did you see it?" Tavian asked. "Did you see the vision?"

Scarlett had to nod. "I saw it. Why show it to me?"

"I owed you an answer." Tavian shook his head. "But it was more than that. I have not shown that to anyone else before, Scarlett. You are special, I feel it, and you need to know. There is a bond between us."

Scarlett pulled back slightly more at those words. She liked Tavian. She had liked kissing him. Even so, she was not going to let him make some kind of claim on her.

"That is not what I mean," Tavian said, obviously sensing her discomfort. "I just mean that there must be something we share, because no ordinary person would have been able to see what I showed you."

The word 'ordinary' took Scarlett's thoughts back to the sight of those two children in the crib.

"You are a changeling," she said. "Cecilia too. The fey… they swapped you for gypsy children."

Tavian nodded. "But I was raised among the gypsies. I was raised human, the way you were."

"What do you mean by that?" Scarlett demanded. "I *am* human. My mother and father are perhaps a little odd, but they are definitely human."

"And yet you saw the vision."

### Supernatural Devices: A Steampunk Scarlett Novel #1

"Well, I have always been able to see the supernatural. That doesn't mean anything," Scarlett insisted. "It isn't like I go around flying or changing my shape. Really, Tavian, what you are suggesting…"

Tavian spread his hands. "I do not want to suggest anything to upset you. I will merely say that Cecilia and I always saw what was really there, too."

Scarlett shook her head. She was not going to unseat everything she knew about her life on the strength of mere supposition. Nor was she going to even contemplate some of the possibilities that came into her head in those moments. There was undoubtedly a simple explanation anyway. Perhaps one of her distant ancestors had been part fey, or something similar. It was far more likely than anything Tavian seemed to be implying.

To change the subject, and because she was not going to give up on her case that easily, she decided to ask the obvious question. "Tavian, if Cecilia knows that she is not Romany, then her story about wanting it as an heirloom of Roma royalty is nonsense. Why did she really take it?"

Tavian sat back down at the table, staring at it for a second or two. Scarlett sat down too.

"Tavian?" she said when he did not speak immediately. "I need to know."

"Yes," he replied, "I suppose you do."

"Then why would Cecilia really have taken it?" Scarlett looked at the young gypsy man. "What is it that I am missing?"

"You have to understand that Cecilia is not a bad person," Tavian said, "but she is obsessed."

Scarlett knew the kinds of things that obsession could do. "What is she obsessed with?"

"With our past," Tavian explained, tracing a pattern on the tabletop. "With what we are. I have come to peace with the fact that we live in this world, but Cecilia thinks that is not enough. She wants to go home."

"Home?" Scarlett found herself thinking of all the legends she had heard when it came to the fey, and particularly about those that claimed they lived in a special land beyond the reach of humankind. "She thought the ring would get her there."

"Exactly," Tavian said. "Everywhere we went, she would ask questions. She would learn the old legends of the faerie folk, and she would talk to those who claimed to

### Supernatural Devices: A Steampunk Scarlett Novel #1

have seen them. She said it was learning about our heritage."

Scarlett cocked her head to the side. "You do not agree?"

Tavian looked momentarily angry. "I have learned some things about the fey, but I learned the most important things when they took away two human children and abandoned us in their place. I was brought up among the Roma. That is what matters. To me, I am human."

"But Cecilia does not think so?" Scarlett asked.

Tavian shook his head. "No. She would talk about finding our real parents. About getting back to our fey home. And if she thought that Darthmoor's ring would help…"

"She would not hesitate to take it," Scarlett finished for him. "Why now, then? I was under the impression that she had worked for Cruces for a while."

"Cecilia started to have visions," Tavian explained. "Ones similar to the one you had just now. They showed her glimpses of another place. She was desperate to get to it."

Scarlett looked at him directly. "And you did not tell me this because…"

"Because at first, it seemed like you might just be working for Darthmoor. I showed you where to find Cecilia, though."

"Yes," Scarlett agreed, "you did." An idea came to her. "And you might just do it again."

She did not give Tavian a chance to ask how as she leaned over the table to kiss him once more. It had to be worth a try, didn't it? After all, if that was what triggered a vision in her the first time, then maybe doing it again would give her some useful information. It wasn't exactly as if it was an onerous way to hunt for clues.

Images did not leap immediately into Scarlett's mind, but she could feel the presence of a second set of thoughts and feelings alongside her own. Tavian's. Thoughts that wanted the kiss to go on forever. That wanted it to be so passionate that Scarlett forgot about the likes of Lord Darthmoor and gave herself wholly to him. That loved the taste of her lips against his, and…

Scarlett fought for control, pulling back from Tavian's thoughts as best she could even as she wondered

### Supernatural Devices: A Steampunk Scarlett Novel #1

how she could possibly learn them like that. Yet she knew that to have any chance of making the connection between them work once more, she could not afford to hold back like that. She had to give herself up to the moment completely.

Scarlett did her best. She kissed Tavian like he was the only man in the world. She kissed him until the establishment around them faded into the background, lost among the intensity of their lips on one another's. Scarlett kissed Tavian deeply, taking everything she could from the kiss, and Tavian kissed her back with every bit as much passion.

At that point, like water from a dam that had finally burst, visions washed over Scarlett. She saw a place that could not be England, with a landscape that was impossible in its beauty. She saw figures roving over it, clashing against one another in waves of flesh and violence. Some were pale, and fast, and as they struck, Scarlett could see their fangs. Others were ethereal and lovely, armed with weapons that held no iron and fighting with every bit as much hate as their vampire foes.

## Kailin Gow

The vision rolled on, and Scarlett saw battle after battle, in a war that seemed to have no end. She saw vampires falling on the homes of the fey with such violence that she would have looked away if she could have done. She saw fey striking back, killing vampires in numbers too great to count. And then she *did* see England. She saw London, and the battles waged in secret around it. She saw that the war was not done, but that it had merely taken a different form in this modern time and place.

More than that, Scarlett saw what she had to do next.

# Chapter 17

Scarlett pulled back from Tavian then. Breathless. He was barely breathing, too, just staring at her with his intense green eyes. She understood more about the war between the vampires and the fey than she had known before. More than that, she had seen places she recognized in that vision, places that were part of the fabric of London.

"I think I can find Cecilia and the ring," Scarlett said. "But we should go now."

"Now?" Tavian repeated. "But why is there such a hurry? As much as I would like to say otherwise, Darthmoor and the boy with the sword might be useful to have around if there is going to be trouble."

Scarlett shook her head. "What I know… it's barely there. It feels like a cobweb. If I leave it too long, everything might fade, and we'll be back to the beginning again."

"So what exactly did you see?" Tavian asked.

Scarlett tried to put it lightly. "Just a few places that Rothschild might be hiding."

"Rothschild? You want to go after Rothschild?"

Scarlett shook her head, standing. "I don't *want* to go after him. I know how dangerous someone like him will be..."

"You don't," Tavian said. "You cannot, or you would not be suggesting this."

Scarlett gripped Tavian by the arm then, a small flash of anger coming out. "Are you suggesting that I should ignore this? The evidence points to Rothschild's involvement, from his augmentation of the Order's mark on me to his standing in less pleasant segments of the vampire community. We have to speak with him."

"So why not just go back to his jewelry shop and speak with him there?" Tavian asked.

"I could be wrong, but... go outside and look for it, would you?" Scarlett waited, and after a second or two just staring at her, he went and did as she asked. It was more than ten minutes before he returned.

### Supernatural Devices: A Steampunk Scarlett Novel #1

"It's gone," the young gypsy man said. "I don't understand…"

"He and those who work for him must have occupied an empty store front," Scarlett explained. "We did not meet by accident. Rothschild went to a lot of trouble to mark me, and to give me his necklace."

Tavian stared down at the sapphire of the pendant Scarlett wore. "You did not say that he had given you that."

"You did not think to comment that I was wearing it after meeting him, but not before?" Scarlett asked.

"I… I did not see it," Tavian said, staring at it again, then lifting the stone lightly in his hand. "There is magic to this. I can feel it now."

"Something to make sure no one noticed it, perhaps?" Scarlett said, and then shook her head. "No, that cannot be all of it. There must be more to the piece, or why insist that I wear it?"

"I do not know," Tavian said, "but I think that you should remove it."

*Do not remove it.* The words sounded in Scarlett's head clearly. *Come to me, Scarlett. You are doing well.*

"I think…" Scarlett struggled to work out the right thing to do. "I think that I should leave it in place for now. And we should go. It will take time to find Rothschild."

Tavian still looked apprehensive at the thought. "Are you sure you want to do this?" he asked. "No one else but you and my sister know what I am. I did not show you that lightly, Scarlett. I… I don't want anything to happen to you."

"I intend to be careful," Scarlett said. "And I intend to find Cecilia. I have no doubt that she will be with Rothschild. It is simply a question of where he is keeping her."

"She might not be his prisoner," Tavian pointed out. "She wanted the ring, and with Lord Darthmoor rejecting her, she might have gone to him willingly. Seeking out one of Darthmoor's rivals would be like Cecilia."

"There is still what happened at the camp to think about," Scarlett pointed out.

"That could have been for your benefit," Tavian pointed out. "It might not have been real. I love my sister, but she can be devious when she wants."

### Supernatural Devices: A Steampunk Scarlett Novel #1

"Then again," Scarlett said, "I will simply have to be careful. Now, we must go."

Tavian, obviously sensing that he was not going to change Scarlett's mind, nodded. "Where are we going? What did you see in that vision that told you where to look?"

"Whitechapel."

"You want to go to *Whitechapel*. That would be dangerous enough even without Rothschild there. Scarlett..."

"Are we going to argue again?" Scarlett asked. If necessary, she would walk out of the public house without Tavian. "I saw vampires collected in Whitechapel. Logic tells us that Rothschild is involved. My talent tells us where he is. We have to go."

"I was merely going to say that I will need to stay close to you in a place such as that," Tavian said. He sighed. "So much for dinner."

They left the establishment and made their way east, first along the river, and then drifting slightly away from it, deeper into the city. They did not take a cab. It was likely that no cab would take them there. Instead, as soon as they were away from the crowds enough not to be spotted, Tavian was able to call up a mist, and they rode it together with the young gypsy man's arms around Scarlett tightly.

The further east they got in the city, the poorer the streets below them became. The stench of the city was noticeable there, and the noise from the streets was clear. Scarlett could see people below in clothes that did not quite fit them, looking thin, ill-fed, and in some cases ill. All that was before they had even reached the limits of Whitechapel Road.

When they did, Tavian landed, and Scarlett forced herself to look around. She was not going to shy away from what she saw, even though what she saw there was squalor on a scale that made her almost ashamed to have the wealth she had. Children sat on the streets, begging openly when they should have been in school. Rough looking men kept wary eyes on the pair of them. Whitechapel was somewhere Scarlett did not think she would have visited by night, but even in daylight, it held a lingering mixture of threat and despair.

"So," Tavian asked. "What now? How do we find Rothschild in this? We cannot just ask around. People in places like this don't tell tales."

Scarlett considered pointing out some of the less than pleasant things people sometimes thought about gypsies, and that Tavian should know better than to label a whole neighborhood like that. At that moment, however, the back of Scarlett's neck began to burn so painfully that she cried out.

"Scarlett, what is it?" Tavian hurried to help her, looking down at her neck. "Your mark, it's glowing."

*Come to me, Scarlett.* As before, the words sounded in Scarlett's head. *Come to me, and come alone. The necklace will show you the way. Bring anyone, and the hostage I have will die. Fail to come, and they die. Hurry.*

"Scarlett?" Tavian asked, putting an arm around Scarlett to support her.

"It's Rothschild," Scarlett said, "and it seems Cecilia definitely is his hostage. He wants me to come to find him. He says that if I do not go alone, he will kill your sister."

Tavian's eyes widened at that threat, but he shook his head. "No, he is lying. It is far too dangerous for you to go alone. I should go with you, out of sight, and…"

"Do you think anything is out of sight in a place like this?" Scarlett demanded, looking around. There were so many spots where watchers could be hidden. We cannot risk Cecilia like that. Your role in this is to fetch reinforcements. Now that we know where Rothschild is, you must fetch Holmes, Cruces, Gordon, and anyone else who can help."

"But I do not know exactly where Rothschild is," Tavian argued, "which means that I will not know where you are."

"You know where to start looking," Scarlett replied. "Please, Tavian, this is the only way it can work."

### Supernatural Devices: A Steampunk Scarlett Novel #1

Tavian stood very still for a few seconds, then he kissed Scarlett briefly but furiously. "Be careful," he whispered into her ear. Before Scarlett could even respond, he pulled back and ran off down one of the adjoining roads. Scarlett watched him go, but not for long, because the pendant around her neck started to move. It swung up, tugging at Scarlett, obviously trying to pull her along behind it like a dog with a scent straining to pull its owner along on the end of a leash.

Scarlett went along with that pull, letting it guide her. Letting it lead her, in fact, much of the way along Whitechapel Road before it pulled to the side quite sharply, directing Scarlett down a small side street. There, on that street, she saw what she knew had to be Rothschild's home.

It was a curiosity shop set into a larger block of homes that arced crazily over the street, looking like it might fall down at any moment. There were items of jewelry in the window, just as there had been before, though here they were joined by other things apparently taken from a hundred different places. Clocks and cabinets, stuffed dead animals and small pieces of art all stacked haphazardly, under the apparently not very watchful eye of a middle aged man. Scarlett ignored him.

She did that mostly because the pendant was pulling her past the clutter of the shop to a door at the back. Scarlett opened it without any complaints from the proprietor, to see a set of stairs leading upwards. At another tug from the pendant, she began to climb. At the top of the stairs…

Scarlett would never have imagined such a pleasantly furnished set of lodgings anywhere in Whitechapel. They put Holmes' rooms on Baker Street to shame, being filled with furniture that seemed to span the centuries in an eclectic mix that took in works in the French and Italian styles along with other, more exotic things. There was a fireplace of solid marble at one side, while comfortable looking chairs marked out a semi-circle around a table that seemed almost Roman in its design. Doors leading off from the room suggested more rooms beyond, but even this one was large enough that Scarlett knew that Rothschild had to have converted the whole block to create this place.

**Supernatural Devices: A Steampunk Scarlett Novel #1**

Scarlett took a step into the room, staring at it, and in the space of the second it took to look around once more, she was no longer alone there. Rothschild was beside her, too close to her, tucking a loose strand of Scarlett's hair back behind her ear.

"Ah, you did what I asked. Scarlett, perfect Scarlett. You are exquisite. Your scent, your beauty. But most of all… most of all, your gift."

## Chapter 18

"My gift?" Scarlett tried not to shudder at the thought of Rothschild so close to her. "How do you know about my gift?"

"I know a great deal about your gifts," Rothschild said, moving in front of her. "So many talents. For seeing the supernatural, obviously, and for other things. Will you come and sit down?"

He led the way to the armchairs, and Scarlett took one of them. She did not know what else to do.

"Are my gifts why you marked me?" she asked.

"Partly," Rothschild admitted, taking the seat across from her. "Of course, it helps that you are exquisite, and that you are able to bridge the gap between the human and the supernatural." He steepled his fingers. "Strange, is it not, that we beyond the human world prize a place in it so highly? Perhaps it is because we are treated as outsiders there so much, when all we do is what nature intended for us. Tea, Miss Seely?"

Without waiting for an answer, Rothschild rose and poured tea from a pot sitting off to one side. He handed the cup to Scarlett. The tea was as excellent as Cruces' had been. Did all vampires make it so well?

"Thank you," Scarlett said.

"I find it pays to be civil," Rothschild replied. "Take marking you, for example. I have done you a considerable favor there, of course. Since you are marked as mine, no other vampire will claim you or mark you."

"It did not stop you," Scarlett pointed out.

"Explain."

"Lord Darthmoor had marked me before you."

"I neither saw nor felt a mark," Rothschild said, and he sounded intrigued.

"And a vampire attacked me before I came to the shop you set up."

"So presumably, he did not feel it either."

Scarlett looked at Rothschild carefully. "That, or he simply had so few manners that he ignored Cruces' mark anyway. But no vampire would do that, *would* they?"

Rothschild raised an exquisite eyebrow. "Cruces and not Lord Darthmoor. My, you must be close. *How* close, Miss Seely?"

Scarlett placed her teacup carefully to one side. "He hired me to retrieve his ring. I imagine you know all about that, though."

Rothschild smiled wickedly. "Obviously." He moved closer to Scarlett then, taking her hands in his and drawing her up to her feet. "Forget Darthmoor. You want me, not him. And you do want me, Scarlett, don't you?"

Rothschild's lips brushed Scarlett's forehead. They made their way down gently, alighting on her eyelids, her nose, her lips. It felt so good. Even though Scarlett knew it was just some form of vampire trick, it felt so very good, so sensual that she almost forgot it was Rothschild she was kissing. No doubt he was putting her under his spell.

"Unhand her!"

That was one voice she had not expected to hear there. "Gordon?"

Scarlett turned, and Gordon was indeed there. His face was red with anger. "Unhand that slut, Rothschild! How dare you kiss her?"

### Supernatural Devices: A Steampunk Scarlett Novel #1

Scarlett blinked in incomprehension. Gordon had never spoken about her like that before. For his part, Rothschild moved over to Gordon, putting his hands on Gordon's arms. "Stop being so rash."

"Rash? You were meant to capture her, not kiss her."

"Gordon?" Scarlett repeated.

Gordon laughed then, and as he laughed, his voice changed, rising in pitch. "So the prim princess is not as clever as she thought." Gordon's form shimmered, changing until it was that of a young woman in layers of silk. Cecilia. "You don't have any talents. You can't even see through a simple glamour."

Scarlett stared at her. "Where is Gordon?" she asked. "You must have seen him, or you would not have been able to copy him that well."

Rothschild moved to take Scarlett's arm, guiding her back towards the armchair. "Have a seat, sweet Scarlett."

Cecilia glared at Rothschild. "Don't you 'sweet Scarlett' her."

Scarlett understood then. "You two are an item? Cecilia, you have had your brother, not to mention the whole of your community, worried about you. I've been looking all over London for you. And you still haven't explained about Gordon."

Cecilia shrugged. "Gordon and I met a week ago at the marketplace. He was buying fresh flowers for your townhouse, preparing it for your arrival. He even asked me if I would be willing to clean it, since the regular servants were in the country. He was rather sweet, letting me look around a house full of your parents' papers and devices like that."

"So what happened to him?" Scarlett demanded.

"Oh, he wouldn't stop talking about you. About how wonderful you were. About how much he longed to see you again. I'm sure you can guess the kind of thing that a young man in love would come out with. So many stories about you that I used to help me glamour into a convincing Gordon."

Scarlett had to smile then, despite her predicament. Gordon liked her in that way? Scarlett would not have

### Supernatural Devices: A Steampunk Scarlett Novel #1

guessed it. But then, it seemed that there was a lot she had not guessed over the last few days.

How long have you been playing the part of him?" she demanded.

Cecilia laughed again. "Since you first saw him back at the house. Oh, I almost skewered Cruces, and he didn't even suspect it was me. I would never have thought I could hold a glamour so long, though."

"That will be your fey blood," Scarlett pointed out.

"You think I don't know that?" Cecilia snapped back. "I've known that most of my life, and do you know, Rothschild is the first person other than my brother who has ever accepted it. The first person who has ever made me feel... loved."

Well, that at least made Cecilia's motives in taking the ring clear. She was one of the Order, or at least worked for them. And all because she loved Rothschild. Rothschild, who had only just been kissing Scarlett. She was not an innocent victim in this. Not by a long way.

"Where are Gordon and the ring?" Scarlett repeated.

"You really think I'm going to tell you that?" Cecilia countered with a contemptuous look.

"No, but I had to give you the chance," Scarlett said. She leapt at Cecilia, slipping behind her even as she drew her dagger, placing the point of it to the other girl's throat. "Now, either you or Rothschild is going to tell me how to find Gordon and the ring. If you don't, then I use this dagger."

Scarlett could feel Cecilia tense with fear. Rothschild, however, merely smiled. "Go ahead," he said. "She is of no further use. Killing her will actually remove a problem from my life."

"Problem?" Cecilia wailed. "I'm a problem to you?"

"You thought I actually loved you, Cecilia?" Rothschild shook his head. "No man wants such a clingy woman, even if she is a pretty little thing. You were a means to an end. My eyes have always been on Scarlett here."

"That can't be true," Scarlett said. "I only found out of you because of the ring."

"Why do you think I arranged for such an obvious path back to me after its theft?" Rothschild asked. "Why do you think I had it stolen here and now? I even saw to it that

### Supernatural Devices: A Steampunk Scarlett Novel #1

an enchantment was placed on you that first night, so that Lord Darthmoor's mark would not take permanently."

"So you felt no mark because you arranged for there to be no mark?" Scarlett asked.

"Exactly."

"Why?" Scarlett demanded.

Rothschild smiled. "All for this. All to get you standing on my carpet here and now, with my mark upon you. You are very interesting, you know. The Order has marked you, and yet they have not killed you. They have not infected you. They know how special you are too. It is why I had to make a personal claim to you."

"Why?" Scarlett repeated.

"I told you before," Rothschild repeated. "Your gifts. All your gifts. After all, you have travelled the world with your parents, finding the items we call simply Devices. Items of power."

Scarlett kept the point of the dagger against Cecilia's skin. "What does that have to do with anything?"

"How did your parents find so many of their artifacts?" Rothschild asked. "You found them for them, didn't you?"

Scarlett wanted to shake her head, but there was a lot of truth to it. Often, she would suggest spots in which to dig to her parents, and there would be things of value beneath. Her parents had told her stories of how she would wander around dig sites as a small child saying "Spoon!" or "Mask!" and there those things would be.

Scarlett was still thinking about that when Rothschild moved, wresting the dagger from her easily and tossing it casually away into the fire grate.

"There, that is much more civilized. We need your talent, Scarlett. We need you to find the Devices for us."

"And the ring is one of them?" Scarlett guessed. It was hardly much of a leap.

Rothschild did not answer then. Instead, one of the doors connecting to the apartment opened, revealing a freakishly tall figure in black. He had to be nearly seven feet tall, and was painfully thin, as well as being completely bald. His eyes were entirely red. Cecilia knew without being told that he was another vampire, but there was nothing beautiful about him. He was simply powerful, and terrifying.

Rothschild bowed. "Welcome, Elder."

### Supernatural Devices: A Steampunk Scarlett Novel #1

The new vampire ignored him. "Yes," he said instead, "the ring is the first. It will open the door, and the Order will enter to destroy what lies beyond." His smile was not pleasant.

"Dastardly!" Scarlett exclaimed. "Of course you wouldn't be using the ring for good, but only for evil." Scarlett knew vampires grew stronger with age, and the most powerful ones were the oldest. Elder must be very strong, if he was named 'Elder'.

Having picked up on Scarlett's thoughts, Rothschild said, "He is one of the most ancient of all of us."

Elder just looked at her. "Come here, child."

Scarlett went. There was no fighting it. She walked over to him and knelt, staring up at him in awe even as she hated herself for doing it.

"Rothschild has been lax. I will not be. Will you join us, girl? Will you join the Order?"

Scarlett clamped her mouth shut to keep from speaking. It was all she could do. However how hard she tried, though, the mark on her neck burned hot enough that she could barely keep from crying out, but she knew that if she did that, she would say yes. Unless there was something else she could shout?

"Cruces! Tavian!"

Elder smiled again. "Ah, Cruces. He should be here for this. He used to be ours, you know."

The pressure on Scarlett relaxed momentarily, so she took the opportunity to ask it. "He was with the Order?"

Rothschild continued. "Cruces practically *is* the Order. He is almost the oldest of us. Older than me. Older even than Elder. The ring was forged soon after he became one of us. His line is ancient and powerful. His father is the father of so many of us, and began the war against the fey."

Scarlett's heart sank at that. Cruces was one of the Order? Had he really been playing a game like that with her all this time? With Holmes? There was no time to think about it, because in that moment, Elder was biting into his own wrist. Blood such a deep red it was almost black bubbled to the surface. Elder pressed his wrist to her mouth.

Scarlett kept her mouth tightly shut. She knew what ingesting a vampire's blood might do to her, and she had no wish to be one of them. Except that, sooner or later, she *would* give in.

"Let her go!"

Scarlett almost sighed with relief at that. The one voice she had been hoping for. Tavian.

## Chapter 19

Still kneeling, Scarlett half-turned and Tavian was there. He held a long wooden spear, worked with sigils that seemed to flow into one another in knots and spirals. He hefted it, and then threw the spear at Elder like a javelin. The spear hit the vampire, but seemed to pass right through him, flashing a brilliant blue as it did so. The same blueness seemed to surround Elder, and he was still, apparently frozen in place.

"That was a fey spear," Rothschild remarked, clearly amazed that Tavian should possess such a thing.

Cecilia seemed almost as surprised, staring at her brother. "You made it through the barrier between worlds? You retrieved a spear?"

"No." That voice was as familiar as Tavian's. Cruces was there, stepping through the door behind the gypsy man. "I just happen to have one hidden away where a thief like you cannot get to it." He pointed at Cecilia.

### Supernatural Devices: A Steampunk Scarlett Novel #1

"You will owe me an explanation, Cecilia. But that can wait, given how briefly the effects of the spear last."

Cruces was over to Scarlett in less time than it took to blink, his hands cool on her arms as he helped her up. He held her tightly, squeezing her hands, his worry over her obvious. Even so, Scarlett knew what she had to ask.

"They said you were part of them. That you were with the Order."

Cruces hesitated briefly, but nodded. "A long time ago, yes. I know better now." He looked over to where Rothschild stood. "I wish I could say the same for you, old friend."

"Friend?" Rothschild said it lightly, but Scarlett could feel the anger there. "You are touching my property, Cruces. I have marked the girl fairly. She is mine."

"Marked her, certainly," Cruces said. "But fairly? In any case, you clearly do not care about stealing what is another's. I would like my ring back now, Rothschild."

Rothschild laughed softly. "Take it if you think you can."

Cruces nodded, lifting Scarlett's hand to his lips, kissing it before gently pushing her towards Tavian.

"Scarlett, go to Tavian, he will keep you safe in what is to come."

Scarlett did not like the sound of that. "Cruces…"

Cruces was already squaring up to Rothschild, violence promised by every line of his expression. When he looked back to Scarlett, his fangs were prominent.

"Go now! I don't want you caught up in this."

"It is a little too late for that, Cruces," Rothschild said. "Scarlett has been caught up in this from the moment it began. Or did you think this was coincidence?"

"He said I was the reason for this," Scarlett explained, from the side.

"You didn't think this was just about your ring, did you?" He reached into a pocket and produced something that shone gold in the light. "After all, I have my own. We need Scarlett more than that, though I must admit that depriving you of the things you want is rather fun, old friend. First your ring. Then the girl. Most enjoyable. I think you'll agree that I owe you that much."

"No," Cruces said. "You don't."

"Cruces!" The vampire aristocrat had been correct about the effects of the spear being temporary. Elder stood as he spoke and threw himself on Cruces. The two vampires fought in a flurry of limbs and flashing fangs, trading blows and slamming one another against the walls of the room with seemingly impossible force. When Elder drove Cruces face first into the wall by the fireplace, Scarlett was surprised that it did not give way completely.

Their struggles were furious, but they also meant that Cruces was no longer in a position to confront Rothschild. Even as Scarlett stepped back towards Tavian, Rothschild pushed past her, lifting the young gypsy man one handed and pushing him back against the nearest wall with his teeth bared. "I believe Miss Seely is with me, not you." He looked over to Cecilia. "Fetch her for me, Cecilia."

Cecilia looked at Rothschild for several seconds, and Scarlett prepared herself to have to protect herself from the other girl. Then Cecilia did the one thing Scarlett hadn't been expecting. She stepped forward and slapped Rothschild sharply. It probably wasn't that hard in vampire terms, but the shock of it was enough for Tavian to slip free, darting past them.

"Why you…"

"That's for how you used me, and that's for my brother," Cecilia said. "How *dare* you discard me like that, you… monster."

Scarlett admired the other girl's fire, but there were more important things right then than telling Rothschild what they thought of him. "Cecilia, where is Gordon? Where is Cruces' ring?"

Cecilia looked like she might say something, but before she could, Rothschild's hands were on her throat. They squeezed with the kind of terrible force that only a vampire could bring to bear, and Cecilia fell to the ground, unmoving.

"No!" Tavian rushed past Scarlett, her dagger in his hand. He had obviously taken it from where it had fallen in the grate, and now he used it to slash and thrust at Rothschild. The vampire was fast, but he clearly knew that the knife could harm him, because he was wary and unwilling to close the distance. He and Tavian darted around in a frantic game of cat and mouse, even while Cruces and Elder continued their wall shaking struggle.

Scarlett ignored both conflicts for a moment, kneeling beside Cecilia, trying to find some sign of life.

### Supernatural Devices: A Steampunk Scarlett Novel #1

One look told her that Cecilia's neck was broken, her throat crushed, but Scarlett sought for some slim sign of life anyway. There was none.

"I'm sorry, Cecilia," Scarlett said softly. "I'm sorry that the people you thought loved you didn't, and that you couldn't see the ones who did."

She stood then, and saw that Tavian was doing well in his fight against Rothschild. He had the vampire hemmed in and was making short, slashing cuts, ready to move in for the kill with a thrust to the heart. After what Rothschild had done, Scarlett would gladly have plunged the blade home herself.

In that moment though, a cry came from Cruces. Scarlett turned, and saw Elder with the fey spear in his ancient hands, while Cruces was surrounded with the faint blue glow that suggested he had been stabbed with it. Cruces was helpless, in no position to resist as Elder dropped the spear and prepared to finish him.

Scarlett reacted on instinct. Without so much as pausing to consider what it might mean, she levered the dagger out of Tavian's hands, gripped it tightly, and leapt towards the spot where Elder's arm was already going back for the killing blow. Scarlett plunged the dagger into his back at heart height, feeling no resistance as the dagger plunged into ancient, paper thin flesh. In less than a second, all that was left of one of the world's most ancient vampires was a pile of silvery dust.

A pile in which something glinted golden. Cruces' ring. Scarlett bent, picking it up and holding it to the light. It was almost identical to Rothschild's. She would have given it to Cruces had he not still been stunned by the spear. Instead, Scarlett held it a second longer.

Heat poured from it, making the metal almost burning hot. Scarlett dropped the ring, then managed to pick it up daintily in her handkerchief. As she did so, Rothschild laughed. He wasn't standing far from Tavian, but he was obviously in no danger now that Tavian did not have the dagger.

"I knew it!" he said, with a level of glee that was almost gloating. "I was the one who told the others in the Order how important it was to find the right girl, and I was right. You are a tracker for us, Scarlett. Every Device you touch will respond to you."

### Supernatural Devices: A Steampunk Scarlett Novel #1

"And through the mark on me, you will feel it," Scarlett guessed. That explained why she had been marked rather than killed, at least.

Rothschild bowed like an actor receiving applause. "Finally, you understand. Oh, Holmes will be so proud when you go back to him. Oops." He put a hand to his mouth theatrically. "You can't, can you?"

Scarlett looked over at the vampire, then at Tavian. "What is he hinting at? Did something happen to Holmes?"

Tavian shook his head. "I do not know. He was not there when I went looking."

"You think he was there at all?" Rothschild countered. "The right actor, with the right glamour…"

"You arranged that too," Scarlett guessed.

"Well, I had to be sure that you would be pointed at the case. Why else do you think London's most famous detective did not clear the matter up in a trice? All that nonsense about you being the only person for the job." Rothschild considered it for a moment. "Well, perhaps it isn't nonsense. You are exactly the right person to do the job the Order wants done."

Scarlett shook her head. "You think I am really going to help you?"

Rothschild laughed once more. "I think you are going to help Holmes and Gordon."

"What have you done with them?" Scarlett demanded. It was hard to keep from using the dagger on the vampire, but if she did so, Scarlett knew that she might not see either man again. It was enough to make her curb her temper, for now.

Rothschild shook his head, and then moved. In less than a second, he was over at one of the doors leading from the room, half out of it and looking back. He glanced at Cecilia with something akin to regret, then, though the expression did not last.

"That is something you will have to find out for yourself," he said. "Of course, since the Order dealt with them in a way that will undoubtedly require the Devices to find them once more…"

"You have created a situation where I have to look for the Devices whether I want to or not," Scarlett finished for him. "You want me to put together the pieces, while you stay consistently just one step behind."

### Supernatural Devices: A Steampunk Scarlett Novel #1

Rothschild shook his head. "Oh no, dear Scarlett. Not behind. Not always. When it comes to the Devices, I assure you that we will be ahead of you, in the end. Now, I should go, because undoubtedly Cruces over there will regain the ability to move momentarily, and I have no fondness for facing superior forces."

"You should get used to it," Scarlett warned.

Rothschild raised an eyebrow. "You actually believe that? And I was starting to have such respect for your intelligence. The Order is large. It is ancient. And it is growing. You are not some raging forest fire to overwhelm us, Scarlett. You are a few points of light that will eventually be snuffed out when you have shown us what we need to see. Farewell."

He was gone through the door before Scarlett could move to stop him. She had more sense than to follow. Rothschild would have a way out, and for now… for now there was Cecilia to consider, along with Tavian's grief, and too many other things to deal with at once. For all that they had recovered the ring, it did not feel much like a victory to Scarlett in that moment.

## CHAPTER 20

The darkness hung about them like a shroud as they stood outside the caravan Tavian shared with his sister. He'd moved it away from the main gypsy camp, partly so that he could be alone with his grief, and partly so that Cruces could travel with them for this last part. Cecilia's body was laid out on the earth before the caravan, and Tavian knelt over her, his tears obvious to Scarlett even in the half light.

Scarlett stayed near him, even though she could feel Cruces' eyes on her. Tavian needed her then, and she wanted to comfort him during his pain. On the way over, Cruces had explained the gypsy way when it came to funerals. When dawn came, Tavian would put his sister's body in the caravan and burn it around her as a funeral pyre. Until then, it seemed, all they could do was be there for him. Even Cruces stood there, his fey spear leaning against the caravan, where he'd placed it "just in case" he'd said.

"I know my sister did many things wrong," Tavian said after kneeling there silently for a while. "I know she did things to hurt both of you, but she *was* my sister, and I will miss her."

Scarlett reached out to put a comforting hand on his shoulder. It didn't seem like enough, somehow.

"I know," she said. "I'll remember her too. There were a couple of moments when I felt like there was some kind of kinship between the two of us. Like we at least understood one another."

Scarlett knelt beside Tavian then, her arm around him. She pulled him close to bury his face against her, feeling the wetness of his tears on her skin.

"I'm going to go and find a drink," Cruces declared, "or it's going to be a long night."

Scarlett saw the look of jealousy that crossed his face as he said it, but right then, there wasn't much she could do about it. Tonight was about Tavian's grief, not about whatever Cruces felt for her. So she knelt with the young gypsy man pressed close to her while Cruces left, slipping off into the dark. She knelt like that for what felt like several minutes, feeling the rise and fall of Tavian's chest against her as he didn't bother to hold back the tears.

Perhaps what happened next was inevitable. Tavian pulled away from her slightly, looking at Scarlett through tear-stained eyes, and then he moved his lips on hers. He kissed her deeply, passionately, with such need that Scarlett found herself swept up in it almost instantly, so that she was kissing him back with fervor. Scarlett knew that the kiss had come from Tavian's hurt, his need for something that wasn't grief, but right then she did not mind. Right then, she wanted it as much as he did. Tavian began moving his hand along her waist, while Scarlett found her hands roaming Tavian's muscular chest.

She had never had a man cry on her before. Her heart reached out to the handsome gypsy man, wanting to soothe away his pain. Despite her attraction to Cruces, Scarlett felt drawn to Tavian, too. He was sensitive, romantic, and straightforward with her. She couldn't help wanting more with him, as their kiss grew stronger, more demanding.

### Supernatural Devices: A Steampunk Scarlett Novel #1

Perhaps that was why neither of them noticed the figure approaching through the darkness until the last second, when Scarlett caught a flash of movement from the corner of her eye. Acting on instinct, she shoved Tavian aside, then rolled clear, just as Rothschild's fangs struck in the space where Tavian had been kneeling.

The vampire looked at the gypsy man with something approaching fury in his eyes.

"She still has my mark on her, changeling. I can sense where she is, feel what she feels. She is mine. Not yours, *mine*."

Scarlett stood, placing herself between the two of them. "I don't belong to you. I don't belong to anyone! You think you can come here and make some kind of claim to me when you have murdered Tavian's sister? Is that what happens to women who get close to you, Rothschild?"

Rothschild looked down at Cecilia's still form and smiled. "Murdered? For a murder, I think you'll find that there has to be a death."

He was still smiling when Cecilia took a rasping breath, gasping as she tried to get air into her lungs, her back arcing with the strain of it.

"Impossible." The word was out before Scarlett could stop it.

"Fewer things are impossible than you might think," Rothschild countered, "and the fey are far from easy to kill. Trust me, I have tried. Without the Devices, it tends not to take. Have you started looking for them yet? You'll need them to get to Gordon and Holmes, remember."

"You've come here, now, for that?" Scarlett demanded. In an instant, she had her dagger out. "Well, at least we know that this will kill vampires."

She slashed at Rothschild. He moved back, and the cut missed. The thrust that followed it cut through his clothing, but appeared to miss flesh. Scarlett lunged then, and perhaps she did it carelessly, because in an instant Rothschild was behind her, one hand forcing the arm that held the dagger out to the side while the other was wrapped around her waist.

"Tell me Scarlett, do you feel what there is between us?"

"The only thing I feel right now," Scarlett replied, "is the urge to kill you."

### Supernatural Devices: A Steampunk Scarlett Novel #1

"Oh, Scarlett, you have no poetry in your soul. There is something electric between us. Why else do you think I waited for Darthmoor to be gone? I've come to fetch you."

Rothschild was pressed tightly to her, and Scarlett could not get free, despite squirming in his grip.

"You are either making fun of me," Scarlett declared, "or you are insane."

"No," Rothschild replied, his grip on Scarlett not loosening in the slightest. "I need you. At the very least, I need you to guide me to the other devices. Believe me, Scarlett, you would prefer that it was me rather than one of the other members of the Order."

"Really?" Scarlett snapped back. "Because right now, it really does not feel that way."

"You saw Elder."

"I *killed* Elder," Scarlett countered.

Rothschild laughed then. "Do you think you can kill all of them? You cannot. And if you keep going on the path you are on, you will find yourself hunted by them. They will do things to you that will make you wish you had gone with me. At least with me, you will be safe."

## Kailin Gow

"Safe?" Scarlett kicked back with her heel. It made no difference. "You think I would ever trust you? You are trying to use me the way you used Cecilia, and look what happened to her."

Cecilia was still on the ground, pulling herself slowly to a sitting position. There was no sign of the damage Rothschild had done to her, but she rubbed her neck nonetheless.

"Don't trust him," she warned. Her voice was a little hoarse, but given that Scarlett had been resigned to never hearing it again just an hour or two ago, it was a massive improvement.

"Oh, believe me," Scarlett said, "I won't."

Scarlett felt rather than saw Rothschild shrug. "Trust me or not, you *are* going to come with me, Scarlett."

He took a step back, but Tavian was there, Cruces' spear in his hands. "You are not taking her anywhere."

"Really?" Rothschild turned carefully so that Scarlett was between him and Tavian. "Yet how are you going to throw that spear without hurting dear Scarlett? I am sure you wouldn't want to hurt her, would you?"

### Supernatural Devices: A Steampunk Scarlett Novel #1

Tavian hesitated, the spear held high, in position for a throw.

"You are wondering if you can strike me without harming her," Rothschild guessed. "Tell me, what do you think the chances are? Whereas if you simply let me take her, she will at least be alive. I'm sure you can see the sense in that, young changeling."

"Let her go!"

Cruces' voice echoed around the space in front of the wagon, seeming to come from everywhere at once.

"Let her go, Rothschild, or you and I will fight, and you would not have waited to come here if you believed that you could win."

"Perhaps I merely wanted to avoid hurting an old friend?" Rothschild countered. "Do not believe yourself to be invincible, Darthmoor. I assure you that you are not."

"Do you want to put that to the test?" Cruces demanded, and Scarlett still could not place his voice. She found herself wondering whether he had really gone off to feed. Perhaps he had, ignoring Tavian's grief because he had known about Cecilia just as much as Rothschild did. Yet perhaps it had been more than that. There was his insistence on bringing the spear to consider, as well as the way he had been close enough to come back when Scarlett was in danger. Had he guessed that Rothschild would try something like this?

"I might," Rothschild said. "After all, she is too valuable to simply give up. You, of all vampires, will know that. But then, perhaps that is why you had her believing this was a real case even though you knew better."

Scarlett looked out into the darkness. "Cruces? What does he mean?"

Cruces came out of the darkness in a blur. He slammed into Rothschild, knocking him from Scarlett, and then kicked him hard enough to send the other vampire sprawling. Scarlett considered following up with her dagger, but it turned out that there was no time. Cruces put an arm around her waist and scooped her up in a single movement. Then he was running; running with Scarlett over his shoulder as he took her away from the forest with almost frightening speed.

"Cruces, what is going on?" Scarlett tried to demand as the vampire ran on, but they were going so fast

### Supernatural Devices: A Steampunk Scarlett Novel #1

she could barely get the words out. Cruces ignored them anyway.

Ahead, there was a road, and on it a cab was parked. Scarlett thought that she might have a chance to find out what was happening once they were both safely ensconced within, but it seemed that Cruces did not intend on merely riding in the vehicle. Instead, he practically threw Scarlett inside, leaping up onto the driver's seat and dislodging the man who sat there with a snarl that sent him scrambling for cover and had the horses rearing.

They did not rear for long though. Cruces whipped them into motion, and then ran them at a furious speed, jolting Scarlett so badly that it was all she could do to keep from cutting herself as she put away her dagger. Cruces drove the cab as though there were demons behind it all the way back to Piccadilly, barely even slowing to avoid the little traffic that was on the streets.

He pulled up outside his house and practically dragged Scarlett from the cab, lifting her as he had back at the caravan then simply carrying her all the way inside. Only once they were in his town house, with the bolt slid shut on the door, did Cruces stop long enough for Scarlett to catch her breath.

"What," she demanded, "was all that about? What's going on, Cruces?"

# EPILOGUE

In the hallway of Cruces' home, Scarlett looked around, trying to make some sense of the speed with which the vampire had taken her away from Rothschild. He had seemed frightened, even terrified. Yet what could possibly frighten something as old and powerful as Cruces? He'd said himself that he was more than capable of defeating Rothschild. Could it be that he was afraid? Of what? Perhaps shortly following Rothschild to Scarlett, many other members of the Order would show up, wanting Scarlett.

"Well?" Scarlett demanded. "I'm waiting for an answer. Are you going to tell me why you just stole some poor cabbie's livelihood?"

"I'll return it before dawn," Cruces promised. "Even if he doesn't put it down to strong drink, his friends undoubtedly will."

"That still doesn't explain why you did it," Scarlett pointed out.

"Come through to the drawing room…"

"I'm not going anywhere until you tell me what's going on." Scarlett put her hands on her hips for emphasis. "Unless you plan on carrying me again?"

Cruces shook his head. "Forgive me for that. It seemed like the quickest way to get you away from Rothschild. I had to make sure that you were safe, whatever it took, and if that meant running off with you in the only chance there was, so be it."

Scarlett leaned back against the wall, looking at the vampire and trying to determine if he was telling the truth or not. She wanted to believe him, but Scarlett was not enough of a fool to believe that liking her would make Cruces any less devious than he had been before. In any case, he still had not answered so many of her questions.

"Tell me about the Order," Scarlett said.

### Supernatural Devices: A Steampunk Scarlett Novel #1

"You know about them," Cruces replied. "You know what they are…"

Scarlett's fist thumped into the wall in a way that was probably completely unladylike. Right then, however, she did not care. "Do not try to deflect me, Lord Darthmoor. Rothschild intimated that you were a part of the Order. Is that the truth? If you will not tell me, I am going to turn around and leave right now."

Cruces stood very still, but he nodded. "A long time ago, I was a member, yes."

"And by a long time, you mean…"

"Thousands of years," Cruces replied. "Yes, there was a time when I was one of them. I believed everything they had to tell me, but at that time, even Rome was nothing more than a village. Egypt and the Greek states were the real powers in the human world. That is how long it has been since I was a part of their madness."

Scarlett tried to think of how long that had been, but she knew that any attempt to truly understand it was hopeless. She had tried sometimes with her parents, when they had unearthed some particularly ancient item. A thousand years was… what? Almost sixty times her lifetime. And Cruces had said *thousands*. The figures were simply incomprehensible.

"You must have seen so much," Scarlett said.

Cruces smiled, and there was a hint of the old humor there. "I find that the modern world has one or two things to recommend it. I really did drag you off to keep you safe from Rothschild, you know. He has a tendency, when he cannot have something he wants, to ensure that no one can."

Scarlett thought back to Rothschild for a moment. "I believe you about that. Thank you for saving me. I believe I will go through to the drawing room now."

Cruces' eyes were on her as she moved away from the wall, the intensity of his gaze undisguised. Scarlett did not have time to think about that for long though, because she found her knees buckling as she tried to walk.

Cruces was there at her side in an instant, supporting her. "It seems that the day has finally taken its toll." He grinned that too irritating grin of his. When he spoke again, his tone was almost mockingly formal. "Will you still object if I carry you, Miss Seely?"

### Supernatural Devices: A Steampunk Scarlett Novel #1

"So long as you're more careful than last time," Scarlett countered. "I swear you bumped my head on the frame of that cab."

"I will be," Cruces promised with surprising tenderness. He lifted Scarlett easily and carried her through to lay her down on one of the sofas in his drawing room. Right then, it felt so soft that Scarlett could almost have closed her eyes and slept, letting the sofa's comfort carry her down into dreams, but there were still things she wanted to know. No. Things she *needed* to know.

"What did Rothschild mean about the case being made up?" she asked, sleepily. "Is this to do with Holmes again? I must admit to being more than a little embarrassed at not guessing what was going on."

"Don't be," Cruces said. "It was expertly done, and it was done specifically with you in mind."

"So what is the truth about Holmes?" Scarlett asked.

"There never was a case involving him," Cruces replied. "I know him, because I am as involved in fighting the supernatural crimes of this city as anyone, but this was never his case. The business with the ring… I involved you for the same reason Rothschild did, because I had heard enough about your gifts to know that they were what I required. I doubt that Rothschild truly has Holmes though. As far as I am aware, he is away on another matter instead."

"So you used me, the same way Rothschild wants to?"

Cruces nodded. "Yes, although I will say that it was with the best of intentions. And I will say that the real work, of tracking down Rothschild and the Order, finding my ring and retrieving it, that was not feigned. I merely disguised it as a minor matter because I could not risk you steering clear of the danger."

Scarlett sat, momentarily affronted. "Do you really think that I would do that?"

"I think your parents might not have given you the option," Cruces pointed out. "Would they really have sent you back alone for something this dangerous? Would they have sent you at all if it had not been for 'Holmes' sending a letter? I cannot imagine that a request from a notorious rake and dilettante for their daughter to assist him would have gone down well."

### Supernatural Devices: A Steampunk Scarlett Novel #1

Scarlett nodded. That made a kind of sense. "What about Gordon?" she asked. "Was Rothschild lying about him as well?"

Cruces shook his head. "We must assume that he was not. Cecilia will tell us the whole story, but for now, we must work on the assumption that Rothschild used his ring to transport the young man beyond this world. It is the only way he would be able to force you to look for the devices, and he would have had to do something to keep Gordon out of the way while Cecilia pretended to be him."

"You know how fantastical that sounds, of course?"

Cruces raised an eyebrow. "Even to you, who can see things others do not?"

Scarlett nodded. "Even to me. Everyone has their limits."

Cruces shook his head. "Believe me, Scarlett, you have not found yours yet. You will see so many other things before this is done. You will go so much further. I almost wish I did not have to ask it of you, but I do, and I must admit, there is a part of me that wants, more than anything, to see what you will become."

Scarlett looked into his eyes, and she knew that the vampire was serious. Whatever lay ahead, it was enough to drive all the taunting from him. Scarlett swallowed. With a quick glance away, she decided to change the subject.

"Rothschild's ring was similar to yours. I saw both it and yours back at his rooms. Now you are suggesting that it can do all that yours is meant to be able to. Why is that, Cruces?"

Cruces sat on the very edge of the sofa. It put him close to Scarlett, but at the same time, so very far away. "The rings were forged together, back in the most ancient days of the vampires. Back when there wasn't even a word for what we were. The eldest of our kind had them forged and gave them to his... children. Five rings, for five vampires, though time has not been kind to all of them."

"What happened?" Scarlett asked.

Cruces shrugged. "All that can happen in those thousands of years. In truth, I am not sure that I even know, anymore. I only know that, where once there were five, now there are only three. They belong to myself, my brother Rothschild, and my sister Lucinda."

### Supernatural Devices: A Steampunk Scarlett Novel #1

"You and Rothschild are brothers?" Scarlett asked, trying to picture the two vampires as such. Somehow, it did not work. There were similarities, certainly, but no, they couldn't be.

"I mean that we share the same maker," Cruces said. "The First. He took us all from our lives, and he gave us the gift he bore. After so long, we are the closest thing to family that each of us has left."

If Scarlett had been unable to comprehend the thousands of years of Cruces' life before, she was totally lost by the idea of three people who had been treated as family for that kind of time. They would be closer than anyone, whether they wanted to be or not. How much could you learn to love others over that kind of time? Scarlett thought back to Rothschild and shuddered. How much could you hate them?

"So what is between you and Rothschild is not just about the Order?" Scarlett asked.

Cruces shook his head. "It is never that simple with Rothschild. Oh, he will want to improve his position in the Order, I have no doubt of that. You may even have done him a favor in that respect by killing Elder. For him though, there is always another layer, and in this case, it is what lies between he and I."

"With me caught in the middle," Scarlett pointed out.

Cruces looked briefly ashamed. "Yes. Please forgive me. If it weren't for me, Rothschild would probably not have put his mark on you. He would not have kidnapped your friend."

"But he would still be trying to find the Devices," Scarlett said, "and for that, he would still need me."

Cruces nodded. "That much is true. We cannot allow the Order to succeed, Scarlett. Their plans call for chaos and the sacrifice of innocents. I have lived among humans a long time. I have seen their brilliance and their foibles, the best and the worst of them. I do not want to see them hurt in the ways that the Order would hurt them if it were to succeed."

"Neither do I," Scarlett agreed.

"And I do not wish to see Rothschild using you like that. Believe me, Scarlett, I would never willingly see any harm come to you. Not from him. Not from anybody. If

**Supernatural Devices: A Steampunk Scarlett Novel #1**

there were another way to do this that did not involve you…"

Scarlett kissed Cruces then, mainly to shut him up, so she thought. But he immediately wrapped his arms around her, pulling her with a kiss that made her toes curl. She kissed him for long seconds before finally pulling back, cradling his head in her hands. "There isn't, though. I believe you, Cruces. Let's stop the Order, and let's find Gordon."

Steampunk Scarlett's adventures continues in Book 2 of Steampunk Scarlett

*Immortal Devices*

December 2011

Kailin Gow

## Sneak Preview from

# Immortal Devices

A Steampunk Scarlett Novel

Book Two

### Supernatural Devices: A Steampunk Scarlett Novel #1

Scarlett sat in the dining room of her family's London home, eating a breakfast that had been brought through by her maid, Frances. The young woman had arrived back from the country just this morning with several of the other staff, and currently seemed to be determined to make up for not having been there when Scarlett arrived by not letting her do anything for herself. Already, she had insisted on helping Scarlett dress in a simple dress of bright blue that went with Scarlett's eyes, and put her blonde locks up in an elaborate arrangement that Scarlett had barely had the patience to sit there for.

The breakfast almost made up for it, though it was ludicrous, having to put up with the formality of a fully set dinner table even when breakfasting alone. Still, at least the tea was well made, the servants having long since learned how important it was to Scarlett. She sat there and sipped it, working her way through the food on the table methodically.

One of the broadsheets sat to one side, but there was little in it to catch Scarlett's interest after the events of the previous evening. In a world full of secret orders and magical Devices, not to mention vampires bent on exploiting those Devices for their own ends, the news that the Empire was in discussions with Germany about reorganizing some of their African territories hardly seemed that important.

Scarlett sighed. She supposed most young women her age in London society would have been happy for an adventure like the one of the last few days to be over. They would have at least welcomed the opportunity to sit down and relax after days and nights spent investigating. They would not have been sitting there, tapping out an irritated pattern on the tablecloth with their fingertips in a way that would almost certainly have drawn a sharp word from her mother had she been there.

Of course, they presumably would not have felt quite so hemmed in by what passed for normal life. They would not have felt, as Scarlett had felt when Frances helped her to prepare for the day, that they were somehow being readied for a part playing the role of the dutiful young woman. What would her day include today? Visiting one of the families she knew in London? Reading some

### Supernatural Devices: A Steampunk Scarlett Novel #1

"improving" book or other? After yesterday, it hardly seemed like enough to fill the time.

Scarlett was still sitting there contemplating that when a knock came at the door. She resisted the urge to leap up and see who it was out of sheer boredom. After all, it was not done for well off young ladies to answer their own doors. Instead, she waited as patiently as she could while Frances hurried off to answer it, muttering darkly about people who called on others so early in the day, rather than at the usual hours for visiting.

It did not take long for Scarlett to detect the sounds of an argument, and less than a minute after that, a figure came barging into the room, pursued by Frances. He was a more than familiar figure, from his long, dark hair to the slightly tanned skin and strong features that made him more than handsome. Scarlett had looked into those Kohl lined green eyes just yesterday, after all. She had stared into them, and even kissed their owner's full lips, getting a vision from doing so in a way that she still wasn't sure she fully understood. It had been a wonderfully `good kiss, too. Perhaps a day ago, that thought might have made Scarlett blush. She did not now.

"Tavian."

"You know this gypsy, Miss Scarlett?" Frances asked with obvious concern. "He pushed his way right past me, demanding to see you."

"Thank you, Frances," Scarlett said with careful restraint as she stood. Would it make any difference to the maid if she knew that Tavian was not just a passing gypsy, but also one of the magical fey, left as a changeling after birth? No, probably not. "That will be all for now."

"You want me to leave you alone in the room with this young man?" Frances sounded almost incredulous.

"That will be *all*, thank you, Frances."

The maid hurried out, and for a moment, Tavian and Scarlett stood there looking at one another. Scarlett took in Tavian's ethereal beauty and for a moment, she wanted nothing more than to rush into his arms…

"Tavian," Scarlett asked, "is everything all right? Please tell me you did not come over just to scandalize the servants."

"No, I… it is better if I show you."

Perhaps Scarlett should have guessed what Tavian meant before he rushed over and swept her into his arms.

### Supernatural Devices: A Steampunk Scarlett Novel #1

The kiss that followed was brief, but passionate. More than that, it brought with it images, exactly the same way that his kiss had let her see so much before. Only this time, it wasn't the long distant past that Scarlett saw.

She found herself standing by Tavian's caravan in the moments after Cruces had whisked her away the night before. How she knew that, Scarlett wasn't entirely sure, but she *did* know it. She could see the almost unnatural good looks of the vampire Rothschild across from her, as well as Tavian's sister Cecilia. Together they looked so similar, with the same dark hair, sharply elegant features and piercing eyes.

She and Tavian were attacking Rothschild in concert. Tavian was lashing out with Cruces' fey spear, which could freeze a vampire in place with a wound, while Cecilia was using a knife that, even if not magical, still looked wickedly sharp. Between the two, Rothschild was having to keep his distance.

Cecilia was talking as she attacked. "You're going to regret using me," she promised, in tones that made Scarlett almost glad that the girl had no reason to hate her too. "First, my brother is going to freeze you, and we'll kill you like the vermin you are. Then, I'm going to make sure that your Order doesn't achieve anything, because I'm going to tell Miss Seely exactly how to find her friend Gordon."

Gordon. Scarlett's longtime friend and fencing teacher, whom she had believed had been helping with the case. It had turned out, however, that Cecilia had been impersonating him using the magic of the fey. The real Gordon had been moved to another world by Rothschild, using one of the magical rings created for the first vampire's "children". The idea had been to force Scarlett into tracking down the magical Devices for him as part of the search for her friend. If Cecilia knew of an easier way to find Gordon…

It was clear though that things were not going to be that simple. Even as Scarlett watched, Rothschild reached out to grab Cecilia, ignoring a thrust of the knife she held and then twisting it from her grip.

"I cannot let you tell her that, Cecilia."

"What are you going to do?" the fey girl demanded. "Strangle me again?"

### Supernatural Devices: A Steampunk Scarlett Novel #1

Rothschild laughed. Even though it was just a memory, and even though she knew what he was now, Scarlett could not help being caught up in the beauty of that sound. "I was thinking of something a bit more permanent, this time," the vampire said.

He lifted his left hand, on which his ring glinted golden even in the moonlight. The air next to him and Cecilia seemed almost to split, tearing like the seam on a badly sewn garment. There was light beyond, so much of it that Scarlett could not see anything beyond that gap. She saw Tavian start forward towards it, knowing already that he did not have the time.

He did not. Rothschild held Cecilia, lifted her, and stepped through the gap he had created as though it were nothing unusual. The gap sealed behind him almost instantly, healing up so that just a second later, it looked like the ragged opening in the air had never been there. Tavian was left simply staring at the empty space where his sister had been.

The vision faded then, leaving Scarlett looking at Tavian from just inches away. She stepped back reluctantly, knowing that even though her parents had little time for the usual formalities and proprieties, they would not like it if someone like Frances were to write to them suggesting that something untoward was going on.

"Where do you think Rothschild took Cecilia?" Scarlett asked.

Tavian shook his head. "I am not sure. It was another world, clearly. Perhaps the world of the fey. It would be an obvious place for them to go, particularly with Rothschild so determined to be rid of Cecilia." His expression grew bleak then. "This is the third time in just days that I seem to have lost her. First when she pretended to go missing. Then, when I thought Rothschild had killed her. Now… now it is hard to know even where to begin looking."

Scarlett reached out to take his hand, ignoring what the servants might think. "We will find her," she promised. "Just allow me a minute or two to get ready."

She headed upstairs, trailing Frances in her wake, and retrieved her Egyptian dagger from her bedside table. Lifting her skirt, she strapped the sheath for it to her thigh.

"Miss Scarlett…" Frances began in a reproving tone.

### Supernatural Devices: A Steampunk Scarlett Novel #1

"Frances, the matter I am about to get involved in may well mean people trying to kill me. Would you rather I were unprotected?"

"But your parents…"

"They gave me the dagger. As for how I have to wear it… well, I admit that it would be a little easier if women didn't have to wear such utterly impractical things, and one day I hope to be able to wear perfectly sensible trousers in the middle of the City…"

"Miss *Scarlett*!"

"…but for now, this is the best I can do. If it makes you feel any better, I am about to pay a visit to an aristocrat in one of the most respectable areas of London. Given the reputation of the aristocrat in question, though, I cannot imagine it is that much of an improvement. Now, would you hand me my coat please?"

Frances did as she was told, thankfully, and Scarlett went back downstairs to meet Tavian.

"Come along then," Scarlett said, offering the young gypsy man her arm. He took it without hesitation.

"Where are we going?" he asked.

"Where can we go?" Scarlett countered. "We need to hunt for your sister in another world. That means using a ring like Rothschild's. There might still be two more extant, but only one of them is in London. We need to talk with its owner."

Tavian did not appear particularly happy at that. "You mean…"

Scarlett smiled. "I mean that we are going to see Cruces, Tavian. Please do try to get along with him this morning. After all, he holds the key to getting Cecilia back."

Supernatural Devices: A Steampunk Scarlett Novel #1

*From Bestselling Author Kailin Gow*

# FADE

What if you find out you never existed…

A stylish, action-packed romance roller coaster thriller of a series with enough twists and turns to keep you guessing.

Available now

Kailin Gow

# Sneak Preview from

# FADE

## Book 1 of the FADE Series™

By Kailin Gow

### Supernatural Devices: A Steampunk Scarlett Novel #1

# ONE

My name is Celestra Caine. I am seventeen years old, which makes me a senior at Richmond High. I never thought this would happen to me, but it has... I'm one of those people you see every day, go to school with, remember seeing at the supermarket or the mall, and then one day you don't hear about them any longer. They're gone, and eventually, you forget them.

Not that I'm easy to forget, as much as I might occasionally wish that I were. I'm tall, about five-seven, and I'm willowy. Built for running, my mom always says. Then there's my hair. It's a bright blonde that always attracts attention, from men and women. The women always want to know what I've done with it, and some of them won't believe that it's simply my natural hair color. The men... like I said, sometimes I wish I didn't attract quite so much attention. Sometimes I think it might be better if I blended in a little more.

## Kailin Gow

It's not all bad, though. My boyfriend, Grayson, loves my hair. He loves touching it, and I love it when he's that close to me. I love it when he gives me that look he has that says, not just that he loves me, but that he always will. That I'm the only girl for him. It's worth standing out a little for a look like that from a guy like Grayson.

I first met him running track- he's the captain of the school team, so it's probably appropriate that I'm at practice with him on the day it starts. Then again, I'm at practice with him most days, so maybe it was always going to work out like that. We finish up, and Grayson invites me back to his place for dinner, but I can't. I have to be home, so I tell him that I'll see him tomorrow and get going.

It doesn't take me long to make my way home, since it's not that far from the school. The house is nice enough, in a neighborhood where there's no trouble, and there are plenty of families around. Dad's car is in the drive, so I guess he must have gotten back early from his work as a biochemical engineer. Mom will be there too by now. She teaches kindergarten, and she's always home before me. Even as I walk through the front door, I can picture her in the kitchen, working away at dinner, maybe yelling at my brother, Bailey, not to spend too much

### Supernatural Devices: A Steampunk Scarlett Novel #1

time online before he's done his homework. It's just how things are in our house.

Except today, something is different. I know that from the moment I set foot through the door. I can't put my finger on it for a second or two, but then I realize what it is. The house is quiet.

"Mom? Dad? Hello?" I call it out, moving through into the living room, then the kitchen. There's no sign of either of them. They aren't there when I check the rest of the rooms on the ground floor, either, which is weird. By 6 pm, at least one of them is *always* there.

Still, maybe it's nothing. Maybe the sinking feeling I have in the pit of my stomach is just an overactive imagination playing tricks on me. For all that I still can't help feeling that there's something wrong, it's not like the place has been trashed, or anything. It's not like anything has obviously been stolen, or is out of place. The opposite, if anything. The whole ground floor is neat, tidy.

Maybe Mom and Dad have just gone next door for a moment. I latch onto that thought, heading upstairs. Bailey will know. He might not pay much attention to things that don't involve computers, but Mom and Dad will at least have told him where they were going.

"Bailey?" I knock on the door to his room, but there's no answer. Telling myself that he probably has headphones on while he's playing one of those online games of his, I invoke big sister's prerogative and open the door anyway.

Bailey isn't there either. And his room's neat. Too neat. Bailey is, like little brothers everywhere, I guess, a one boy disaster zone. This looks like one of those occasions when Mom has finally gotten tired of telling him to clean his room and done it for him, which means that Bailey can't have been back since.

In fact, the whole house has that feel. Like someone has scrubbed it from top to bottom, and no one has been in it to mess it up yet. That probably doesn't sound like a big deal, but for me, it's enough. Enough to send me hurrying around the house, looking for clues as to what might be happening. Because there's *something* happening. I'm certain of it.

I go to search every room again, even though it doesn't make sense. After all, Mom and Dad and Bailey aren't about to leap out from behind the sofa, are they? There's still no sign of them. More than that, beyond the car in the drive, there's still no sign that any of them has even been home.

### Supernatural Devices: A Steampunk Scarlett Novel #1

I check my messages. Maybe there's an explanation there. There's nothing. There's nothing when I check my emails, either. Not even the usual stuff I'd get most days, which only makes me bite my lip harder with the worry of it. I don't like this. I *really* don't like this.

Should I call the cops? That thought springs into my head from nowhere. What would I tell them, though? That something doesn't feel right in my house, and that it looks like a team of cleaners has been through the place? They'd laugh at me, or worse, accuse me of wasting their time.

I haven't called my parents yet, so I try that next. I get out my cellphone and call the number for my father. It doesn't even ring. Instead, I just get this message, saying "Error, number not recognized."

The same thing happens when I call my mother, and when I try to connect to the number for the cellphone Bailey has 'for emergencies'. I've sometimes wondered what kind of emergencies a ten year old can have. I guess now I know. I'm breathing faster now, and I know I'm starting to panic. This kind of thing just doesn't happen in D.C. Not that I know what "This kind of thing" is yet.

## Kailin Gow

I punch in another obvious number. That of my Aunt Chrissie. She's my mother's sister, and my parents always say that if anything serious happens, and they aren't around, I should ring her. I'm not sure what good it's meant to do, ringing a woman we hardly ever see to come and ride in to save the day, but right now, I'm willing to try anything.

"Error. Number not-"

"Stupid thing!" I throw my phone and it bounces off the sofa, coming to rest on the carpet. I stand there seething with anger at it for a minute, my head spinning as I try to make some sense of all this. There has to be a logical explanation for all of it, right? People don't just... disappear.

Only, I can't think of an explanation that works. Unless I'm willing to believe that my parents and brother have all chosen to call in on one of the neighbors together right at the moment when a freak fault has developed in my phone, and what are the chances of that?

This is really starting to weird me out. So much so that I can barely breathe with it, while my stomach is tight with the apprehension running through it. Nothing good is happening. I'm certain of that now. I just wish I were as certain about what to do next. I need to calm down. To think.

### Supernatural Devices: A Steampunk Scarlett Novel #1

Grayson. I latch onto thoughts of him like a life preserver. He's always been my rock; always been there for me. Whenever I panic about not getting good enough grades to make the track scholarship to Georgetown, he's the one who talks me through it and helps me study. When I'm down about my track times or just annoyed with my little brother, he's the one who picks me up.

Even though this feels so much more serious than that, I snatch up my phone and speed dial his number. For once, I don't get that stupid message, either. Now all I need is for Grayson to pick up.

Come on, Grayson, pick up.

He answers on the fifth ring, though given how fast my pulse is currently racing, it feels far longer.

"Hello?" he asks. "Celestra?"

I'm so happy to hear his voice in that moment that I can't think of anything to say. There's too much of it, and it all sounds so crazy. There's the house, and the emptiness, and the stuff with my phone. For a couple of seconds, all I can do is stand there, listening to him on the other end of the phone like some kind of weird stalker.

"Celes, is that you? Are you all right?"

## Kailin Gow

His use of that pet version of my name snaps me out of it. This is Grayson. I can tell him anything, even the strange stuff. He'll find a way to make all this make sense, or at least a way to make me feel better about it. I open my mouth to explain. To simply say his name.

Before I can get the words out, my cellphone dies. Just dies, without an explanation. There's no power, even though I'm sure I charged it up this morning. It won't turn on, it won't light up, and it certainly won't let me say anything to the one person who might be able to help me. I stand there, just staring at it dumbly, for a second after a second.

The main house phone starts to ring in the kitchen. It's an old thing my dad liked the look of and had rewired, even though we all have individual cellphones. The ring is harsh, cutting through the silence of the house in a way that only emphasizes it.

Has Grayson called me back on the house number, guessing what has happened to my phone? That must be it. I rush through to the kitchen, knowing that I have to talk to someone about this, or I'm going to burst. I snatch up the handset, cutting off that sharp ringing.

"Hello?"

## Supernatural Devices: A Steampunk Scarlett Novel #1

"Celestra Caine?"

A man's voice. It's not Grayson. It's not anyone I know. And yet, whoever he is, he obviously knows me. Coming here and now, I know the call has to have something to do with whatever is going on.

"Who is this?" I ask.

"Celestra Caine, you are about to fade."

******

FADE (Book 1: FADE Series)
Available Now

Kailin Gow

From Bestselling Author Kailin Gow comes

# DESIRE

A Dystopian world where everyone's future is planned out for them at age 18…whether it is what a person desires or not. Kama is about to turn 18 and she thinks her Life's Plan will turn out like her boyfriend's and friend's – as they desired. But when she glimpse a young man who can communicate with her with his thoughts and knows her name…a young man with burning blue eyes and raven hair, who is dressed like no other in her world, she is left to question her Life's Plan and her destiny.

Available Now

Supernatural Devices: A Steampunk Scarlett Novel #1

Want to Know More about the *Steampunk Scarlett Series*, Author Insight, Author Appearance, Contests and Giveaways?

## Join the Steampunk Scarlett Official Facebook Fan Page at:

http://www.facebook.com/SteampunkScarlett

**Talk to Kailin Gow, the bestselling author of over 80 distinct books for all ages at:**

http://kailingow.wordpress.com

on Twitter at: @kailingow